NOOKIE'S SECRET

Anieshea Dansby

Published by
Art Official Media LLC
PO Box 39323
Baltimore, MD 21212

ISBN-13: 978-0-9768061-2-7
ISBN-10: 0-9834874-0-5

Library of Congress Control Number: 2011925718

Cover Design: Candace K Designs

Editor: Q.B. Wells

For information regarding special discounts for wholesale purchases, please contact the sales department books@ArtOfficialMedia.com or phone 443.693.7622 fax 443-378-7081.

Books by Anieshea Dansby
Nookie by Anieshea Dansby
Nookie's Secret (Nookie 2) by Anieshea Dansby
Read the excerpts online. www.ArtOfficialMedia.com

Address inquiries to:
Art Official Media LLC,
PO Box 39323
Baltimore, MD 21212

CHAPTER 1

For three months Joy and Dre stayed at the Miami Beach Resort & Spa. Since their arrival Joy loved everything about Miami. She was most excited to see the Atlantic Ocean out her front room window. Everything around her fascinated her, having been nowhere other than New York City, Jersey and Philly. The room had a living area as large as her boyfriend Shawn's apartment with blue and white suede furniture. There were two bedrooms, one room had the largest king size bed Joy had ever seen. The sand on the beach was white and Joy stared at it for a longtime, running her fingers and toes in it.

Joy's days were filled with going to the Spa every morning and snorkeling, Jet skiing, deep sea and surfing, scuba diving, parasailing and windsurfing. She played golf, tennis and beach volleyball.

After a few weeks Joy did everything more than once and ventured further, taking daily cabs to shops at South Beach. She went in every store on the "Fifth Avenue of the South" strip. She had more bags from Gucci, Prada, and Dolce & Gabbana then she could carry. She needed help from the bellboy when she got back to the hotel.

Joy and Dre became close over the few months they had been in Florida. He became like the brother she never had. Joy let her guard down. She respected Dre because he never came at her wrong and always was nice. But lately, he'd been acting stranger and stranger by the day. He refused to do any of the activities with her. She begged him to ride to the Miami Metro Zoo. She wanted to share the experience with him because she never had the opportunity when she was little. She ended up going by herself. Dre slept that day, went out that night and didn't return until dawn the following day.

Joy got tired of eating out and chilling by the pool. She wanted to leave and get an apartment somewhere in Miami. Dre thought an apartment would make them hot. Joy attempted to reason with him that someone would be willing to take cash, no questions asked. She worried about the money they spent going out, with nothing coming in. Sooner than later they would need more money.

Joy sat in the living room with a duffle bag in front of her. The money that she and Dre stole was divided into $167,150 a piece and left in the bag. The bag held a little over 20,000. Joy knew that she didn't spend that much money on clothes and fun activities. She kept all her receipts and wrote what she spent on a piece of notepad paper. The room was a package deal that they paid on arrival and had to pay a small fee for each additional week. The only extra money needed was at the spa, food and tip.

The anger and rage inside of Joy boiled in her chest every time she looked down into the bag. At first, she tired to reason that maybe he put it up so that in case housekeeping found it, it wouldn't be a total lost. The money wasted surprised and angered her more. She couldn't trust him. "If he was so honest, why wouldn't he let me know?" She thought. What if he left and wasn't coming back?

She got up and began to pack her stuff. She went to the hotel gift shop and brought three suitcases to pack her new clothes. After that was finished, she placed the bags in the second room under the bed where she knew that Dre wouldn't look.

As soon as she closed the door behind her, Dre shot through the front door, sweating, and breathing hard. He plopped down in one of the chairs. He closed his eyes and opened them to find Joy staring.

"What?"

"What you mean what?"

"Why you looking at me like that?"

"What's up with you?"

"What you mean?"

"You come running in here, looking all crazy."

"Ummm, I took the stairs because it was too many people waiting for the elevator."

Joy sat back down in her seat, the duffle bag on the floor. Dre followed her with his eyes on the duffle bag. His eyes widened and he looked like he was about to bolt.

Joy asked, "Dre where's the rest of the money?"

"Oh, it's in the hotel's safe. I meant to tell you, I was worried about some one stealing it from the room."

"How could you not tell me? Maybe I don't want them holding my money."

"Joy, it's cool I will get it tomorrow."

Joy watched his eyes shift around the room and knew he was lying. The money was gone. "You don't think the hotel would become suspicious about the money?"

"No, it's cool Joy." Dre said irritated.

"Okay. How about I order room service?"

"Yeah. Get me bacon, sausage, eggs and cheese grits."

Joy went to order the room service. When she hung up the phone, she grabbed her purse and went to the bathroom. Before she closed the door, she glanced at Dre one more time. He had his head back and was still breathing heavy. She sat down on the toilet and rummaged threw her purse. She pulled out a small plastic sandwich bag. She looked at the contents and wished that it could be different. Just once she wished she could find someone honest to ride out with her.

Before she left Philly, she took with her a container of rat poison she found under Shawn's sink. She placed the poison in her bag and planned to use it on Dre at the first opportunity. But when her and Dre became so close she changed her mind. She regretted that now.

Taking the container out the bag, she poured some of it into the plastic bag and put the bottle back in her purse. She would get rid of it later. She planned to place it in Dre's food. His death would be slow and painful but Joy didn't care: the hotel would be at fault because he ate their food.

She heard a knock at the door. She stuffed the bag in her jean pocket and made her way out the bathroom. Dre was still in the same position. She heard someone shout room service. She didn't bother to look. Opening the door wide enough for a food cart, four men stormed through. Before Joy could speak one of the men grabbed her and put his hand around her mouth.

"Tie this bitch up," the man said in an accent.

Two other men tied her hands and feet then sat her on the sofa. They went over to Dre who didn't move. They tied him up, stuffed rags in their mouths, and wrapped duck tape around their heads.

Joy squeezed her eyes shut and tried to think of a way out. She had a sinking feeling but was determined not to die. There was no telling what the men would do.

CHAPTER 2

Joy struggled and forced open her eyes. She looked across at Dre, tears and snot poured down his face. She felt disgust for his weakness that and she wished they killed him first so she could watch. The situation was his fault. He did something, she didn't know if it was gambling or drugs but they were tied up for a reason.

Closing her eyes again, Joy prayed that God would rescue her from death. She had never been introduced to any religion, but she believed that there was a God. She hoped that *He* would save her.

One of the men walked up to Dre, pulled out a .45 and pulled the trigger. Joy heard a faint noise only a little louder than someone spitting across the room. She heard the thud as the bullet entered Dre's forehead. Her heart began to jump in her chest. If the gun had a silencer on it that meant nobody would've heard the shot. She had no chance of someone coming to rescue her.

The men stuffed Dre's body into a suitcase. One of the men walked over to Joy, shook his head and raised the gun to her head. One of the older men noticed and came over and in a Russian accent said, "Don't mess up her pretty face so she can have an open casket.

The one holding the gun lowered it to her chest. Joy shut her eyes. A bright light flashed and then there was darkness.

11

"Ahhhhhhhh." Joy screamed; waking up to Dre slamming the car door at the same time she got shot in her dream. "That shit was a dream." Joy said stunned, wiping the cold out her eyes. Rain tapped the window, lightning flashed, thunder roared right behind it. Joy didn't know where she was. Could the whole thing be a dream? She wiped her eyes and looked out in front of her. She noticed an illuminated Wawa sign and saw Dre in line. Behind her she saw the gas station pumps with attendants pumping the gas.

Dre returned to the car and tapped a pack of Newport's against his hand before pulling one out. He offered the pack to Joy who took one. He lit hers, then his and started the car.

"Where are we?"

"Chester."

"That's it?"

"What you mean? I've been driving for like 45 minutes."

"It seems longer."

Joy laid her head back and thought about how real the dream she had seemed. It may be a warning. She studied the side of Dre's face.

"You must've been tired. You was snoring and shit..."

"Yea."

"What's wrong with you?"

"I was thinking maybe we should go some where else."

"Why? What's wrong with going to Miami like we talked about." he rubbed up and down her thigh.

Joy fought the urge to move her leg, so Dre wouldn't know that she didn't want him to touch her ever again.

She leaned back farther in the seat and tired to still the crazy thoughts running thru her mind. The night she ask Dre to help her set Shawn up ran thru her mind.

Dre came over to meet up with Shawn, who was running late. Joy let him in and they both sat on the sofa waiting for Shawn. Scared of how Dre would react knowing he was Shawn's boy, Joy almost chickened out. After only a few seconds of thinking this, Joy took a deep breath and blurted out, "Yo, I know where Shawn stashes his money."

"Yeah? He told you that?"

"Yeah."

"What you telling me for?"

"I thought you might want to know." Joy began to think she fucked up, when Dre asked, "You got a plan?"

"Not really." Joy shrugged her shoulders. Hoping Dre would show some sign that he was with it.

Dre looked at Joy with a puzzled look and said, "You playing, right?"

"No."

"Alright. So you're saying that you know where the money at, why you just don't take it and leave?"

"Look, are you going to help me or not, because I can't have Shawn coming after me." Joy yelled; worried Shawn would come back before Joy knew if Dre was down or not.

"Yeah."

Joy took another deep breath. Dre did most of the talking from there, telling Joy what was going to happen and who he would get to help him.

As soon as the two hashed everything out: Dre's phone rung. When he hung up, he said that Shawn changed his mind and that they would meet up later at Rob's house. Joy got up and walked Dre to the door.

"Before I go, we have to seal the deal." he cheesed.

"What?"

Next thing Joy knew, Dre had her pinned against the door giving her a wet and sloppy kiss. Caught off guard, Joy just stood there. She then tired to follow his rhythm but that didn't work. Finally, she turned her face and he began to kiss her neck and unbutton her pants. "Take them off," he demanded. And she did, along with her panties.

Dre unzipped his zipper and pulled out his dick. Joy quickly looked down to see what he was working with. She didn't see anything at first glance. She looked down again and saw the head of a very small dick. She almost sucked her teeth but thought twice about it.

He lifted her up and she wrapped her legs around his waist as he entered her. The only thing Joy felt was his zipper scratching her pussy. "Shit." she said. Dre took that to mean she liked it and sped up. Joy tried to tell him but he came. Sweating, face scrunched up his body jerked and Joy would have laughed if her pussy didn't hurt. Dre tapped her ass and grinned. He zipped up his pants and left.

"Joy, Joy..."

"Huh?"

"You good? You never answered. I thought you was sleep again, until I saw your eyes open."

"Yeah. Just thinking."

"Bout what? You not worried are you?

"Naw. I just have some stuff on my mind."

"Oh." he sounded hurt but Joy ignored him.

16

Joy began to regret asking Dre to help her. The knots in her stomach that appeared after her dream further convinced her of this. She had to find a way to get away from him. He would bring her down and she couldn't have that. The past few months of Joy's outlook on life had changed. She went from a sheltered young girl to a woman on a come up. She thought of Kevin. She wondered what he was doing. She tried to forget him but now she wished he was present.

Joy looked over at Dre, who concentrated on the road. A plan formed in her head to get away from him. She took a deep breath and tried to get enough courage to go through with it.

CHAPTER 3

Joy's entire body felt hot, her head throbbed and her blood pressure was up because of what she was about to do.

"Can we stop? I have to pee."

"Alright."

Dre drove a little farther down the road before he reached a gas station with a restroom. They both got out the car and went to the bathroom. Joy opened the door, the stench of mold and urine hit her dead in the face, almost making her turn and leave. She felt Dre behind her and stopped, causing him to bump into her.

"What you doing?"

"I thought I could get some head right quick." he said, with a stupid grin; closing the door. Dre didn't wait for an answer. With one hand he unzipped his pants as he pushed Joy to her knees. With a heavy heart, she took his tiny dick into her mouth. It didn't even reach her throat.

After only three minutes, he cum filled her mouth. He didn't help her up. She got up and spat his cum on the floor. With his pants still down, he walked to the toilet and peed all over the place. Joy turned her head away.

"I'm going to the car to get a tampon out my bag." After she said that she realized that she couldn't remember the last time she had her period. "Shit" she thought. But she couldn't worry about that now.

"Uh huh." was all he said, still relieving himself.

As soon as the door closed behind her, she ran to the car. She opened the driver side door; she grabbed her pocketbook and opened the trunk. She closed the door grabbed the backpack with the money. She looked back at the bathroom door to make sure Dre wasn't coming. She peeked through the gas station window; the clerk was helping a customer. Bag in hand, she ran to the other side of the station. She searched around for a place to stash the bag until later. She found an old recliner. She opened it up and stuffed the money and her bag under the seat and closed it back. Her plan was going to happen sooner than she thought.

Joy panicked thinking that Dre was out of the bathroom and at the car. She didn't know when she would have another opportunity to get away. Her breathing became short, making it hard for her to breath. She peeked around the corner to see if Dre was in the car. Surprisingly, he wasn't. *"Not in the store either. He must be taking a shit,"* she said aloud to herself. Time to put her plan in motion. She ran her fingers through her shoulder length hair to give a wild look. Knowing that wouldn't be enough, she repeatedly smacked herself in the face until her face stung and felt swollen. She could tell that it had to be red because of how hot her skin felt. She took her sneakers off and threw them behind the chair. She ripped her shirt at the bottom and unbuckled her pants.

She then ran to in the store, behind the counter to the clerk. "You have to help me," she screamed, wild eyes. Tears running down her face.

"What happened to you? I'll call the police."

"Please." Joy said crying harder.

The clerk already had the phone in his hand, told the person, "I will call you back." and began dialing the police.

Out the corner of her eye, Joy watched Dre walking towards the car. Joy ducked down and watched Dre go to the car, noticing it was empty; he looked on direction to the store. The clerk who was off the phone, looked down at Joy, confused.

"That's the man who hurt me." Joy pointed toward the door that Dre just walked in.

The clerk becoming nervous, pushed Joy more under the counter and stood in front of her trying to hide her. Joy held her breath and tried to calm down. She was so scared that Dre would see her that she began to shake.

"Did you see a girl like 5-5, brown skin?"

"No, it's been pretty dead in here." the clerk said, cutting Dre off.

Dre walked out the store mumbling, "racist muthafucka." thinking the clerk was being short with him because he was a racist white man. Joy peeked out from the counter. Both her and clerk watched Dre get in the car, he sat there for two minutes before he started the car. Then something must have dawned on him. He jumped out the car and ran to the trunk. He tried to pull it open. He ran back, popped it open. "Fuck." he yelled at the top of his lungs. "Joy you dirty bitch." He pulled the gun from his waist. He heard some cars pull up and car doors slam. Before he could turn around he heard, "Freeze. Drop the gun."

CHAPTER 4

Dre's heart sank. He didn't know why the police showed up but he guessed it was Joy's doing. He knew that he had no way out of this because the gun he brought off his cousin might have bodies on it. He was glad he dumped the other guns he used after robbing Shawn. All these thoughts ran through his head in the three seconds between the cops pulling up and them repeating for him to "drop the gun."

The cops took Dre's no response as a threat, and opened fire.

Joy watched from behind the counter, as Dre's body jerked and fell against the hood of the car. The clerk was so engrossed in what was happening, he didn't notice the young woman he went out of his way to help, slip from behind the counter and into the back of the store. She looked over her shoulder to see if the clerk noticed. He hadn't. Finding the back room, she entered and noticed an exit sign over a door. Joy went to the exit, peeked out and after seeing no one stepped outside.

Once outside, she took a deep breath. She heard the police walkie-talkies and her heart pounded. Lifting the chair out, she looked down at the bag with the money. She reached down to pick it up, when she heard, "What are you doing back here?"

Joy turned around to face the voice. A tall and skinny, young white dude wearing a smock stared at her.

"Shit, why you sneaking up on people?" she replied, reaching down grabbing the bag and her sneakers. She reached in and took a few bills from out of one of the rolls of money and handed them to the dude. She put her finger to his lips, as if to say shush, leaving him there with his mouth open. He looked down at the few hundreds in his hand, placed them in his pocket and walked off.

Joy continued down the road, hoping the police weren't looking for her yet. She knew that they would want to know what happened. The thought of having to talk to the police again made her walk faster. No cars passed and that made Joy wonder what the time was. Since she knew she was close to Philly, she needed to find a bus stop. With no clue to as where to go, she walked.

Flipping open her phone she saw that it was almost midnight. Joy began to think that she should have come up with another plan of getting rid of Dre. A plan that didn't include her hungry, tired and in the middle of nowhere. She wasn't surprised that she didn't feel the least bit sorry that the police killed him.

Joy opened the bag and took out a couple of rolls of money and put them in her pocket book. She looked around before placing the bag on her back. Finally, she thought when a car coming her way, she could find a way out. The car slowed down as if to help her but passed right by her. When cars began to pass frequently Joy felt like she maybe close to a highway or maybe a bus stop.

One of the drivers beeped the horn and Joy looked back to see that he had pulled over. She kept walking, not wanting to get in a strange car but she thought about how long she been walking. The car moved forward about to pull off. Joy ran a little. The driver noticed, waited for Joy to come to the car. Joy went to the open window and looked in.

Inside was a middle age woman, with a warm smile. Joy was surprised and relieved that it wasn't a guy. It clamed her nerves and Joy got in and relaxed in the seat.

"So where you headed?" the woman asked.

"I was hoping to get back to Philadelphia."

"Oh, I headed that way. That's not that far. What's your name?"

"Joy."

"Joy. I like that. I'm Brenda. So where in Philly are you going?"

"It doesn't matter. You can drop me at a bus stop."

"No, I'll take you where you got to go. It's getting late and the streets aren't safe. I don't mind driving. I actually enjoy it. I just came from Harrah's casino."

"Oh." Joy not really paying attention.

"Yeah. I lost my rent money but I had a good time."

"Damn." Joy looked out the window. The road seemed familiar. "Is this Roosevelt Boulevard?"

"Yeah."

"I'm headed to Frankford. I don't know how I'm going to tell my daughter I lost seven hundred dollars."

Joy shook her head. A little irritated with the lady talking about the money she lost.

"I only live right over there in Frankford, you can spend the night. I have an extra room." She hesitated, and then said, "It is kind of late."

"Umm." Joy didn't know what to say. She thought that maybe it was a hint that she was too tired. "Okay." She didn't like the idea of staying at her house. She figured she could handle her if it came down to it.

"Good."

They rode the rest of the way in silence. Five minutes later they arrived at a three-story building. Brenda parked and led Joy through the building. Joy was nervous because the hallway was dark. She flicked a switch and everything lit up. Right in front of them was a staircase but Brenda led them to a door on the right.

Opening the door, she let Joy go first. Joy stepped in and looked around. It was clean but cluttered with too much furniture and stacks of opened mail.

"The bathroom is right there to your left and where you'll be sleeping is back here."

She led Joy to the back of the apartment where there was two bedrooms. She opened the door. Joy quickly looked in and noticed a made bed and television.

"Thank you so much for letting me stay here tonight."

"No problem. Goodnight."

"Goodnight."

Brenda walked back towards the living room. Her bedroom must have been the door Joy noticed to the right when she walked in. Joy went in the room and shut the door behind her. Sadness swept over her. Here was someone else, helping her. Tears swelled in her eyes but she refused to let them fall. Her throat burned and she had to swallow to wet her throat and relieve the sensation.

She took her shoes off and lay across the bed. Joy felt lost. She thought of Kevin but she realized that she didn't think about him as much any more. Maybe she didn't care about him after all. She wanted to feel loved but when she may have had it with Kevin, she messed it up.

And when Shawn showed her that he cared about her she had him robbed and murdered. She blinked to get rid of the image of his dead body in the bathtub with a bullet hole in his head. For the first time, she thought about the murder. She thought about Shawn's little boy who would grow up without a father and it hit her. She was destroying the love of the people that Shawn, Josh and Dre loved and those who loved them. In some sick way she was showing them her pain.

CHAPTER 5

Joy opened her eyes for what felt like the thousandth time. She knew at least an hour passed and still she was unable to sleep. Her body felt exhausted and she hardly wanted to move. She needed to leave. She had something on her mind and she had to handle it.

She reached in her bag and began counting the money. There were twenties, hundreds, tens, fives and one. When she was done, she was speechless. The amount she counted, adding the money she gave dude outside the store came to 334,300. Which was way less than the little over 500,000 Dre quoted earlier. She was happy since she never had this much money in her life. Plus, she didn't have to split it with Dre any more. That thought made her think of something else. Picking up the pen and paper she used to calculate the money amount, she divided the amount in half.

"Shit. 167,150. Just like in the dream," she thought to herself.

She couldn't believe it. The dream was trying to tell her something after all. She flipped the paper over and began to make a list of things she needed to do. She needed a car and a place to live. *Where*? She wasn't sure. Maybe New Jersey or maybe she'd go back to New York. She had people she knew there and she wouldn't be totally alone. It would be easy for her to get an apartment.

Joy counted out a stack and laid it on the bed. She gathered the rest of the money and her belongings and placed them all in her bag. She put her shoes back on and opened the room door. It was too dark to see. Slow, she moved with her hands out. It was a straight shot to the living room. She found the door, cracked it open and went out and closing it behind her. She went through the second door and let out the breath she was holding. She really hated to sneak out like that but she wasn't for all the questions when she didn't have any answers. Joy always had been very impulsive; something she needed to try to control.

She sat down on the steps, just now remembering that it was late and none of the buses were running. Joy got up and walked towards Frankford Ave. Once she reached the corner, she looked around. No cars were in sight, so she kept walking towards Bridge and Pratt.

The night air felt good on her face. She continually looked behind her to make sure nobody snuck up on her. She had all this money in her bag and she decides to go after three in the morning. A car drove by, the driver horning at her. She ignored him and kept up her pace. A hospital sign caught her attention and she walked towards it. When she got close enough, she saw that it was Frankford Hospital.

Joy walked inside and saw that no people were in the waiting room. She went over to the payphone and opened the phone book to look for a cab company. When she found one, she dialed the number from her cell phone, despite the no cell phone signs posted throughout the waiting room.

The wait for the cab wasn't long. Not even ten minutes later, the cab driver was beeping the horn for her to come out.

Once inside the cab, Joy gave the driver the directions and hoped that she was making a wise decision.

CHAPTER 6

Joy looked up at the building she had the cab driver let her off at. She knew his new address because he had somehow got her cell phone number and left her a message letting her know where to find him, if needed.

She looked for his name among the bells. She pressed. No answer. She pressed it again, a little longer.

Finally, she heard a groggy, "What the fuck you want?"

"It's me, Joy."

"Oh my God, Joy?"

He buzzed her in and she went inside. She took the elevator to his fourth floor apartment. He was standing in the hallway waiting for her. When she made it close enough to him, he grabbed her and hugged her. Joy stood there, confused by his strong display of affection. After all, she just recently met him and found out he was her estranged uncle Curtis. And then shortly after that found out he wasn't her uncle because her father wasn't even her father.

"Come inside." he pulled her inside his apartment before she could move.

"Sorry to bother you but I need your help."

"No problem. I was so worried about you since what happened to your parents. And with everything you found out all at once."

"Well you don't have to be because I'm doing okay. I been doing a lot of thinking about the shit I've been through lately………" Tears raced down her face and Joy stopped mid-sentence.

"Look sit down over there and I'll get you some water."

Joy went over to the sofa, sat and waited. She used the back of her hand to wipe her tears. She couldn't believe how choked up she wasn't getting. The feeling to cry has been present strong lately. Curtis returned with a glass of water. After drinking it down in a few gulps, Joy got up and went in the kitchen and poured herself another one. Returning into the living room, she started over.

"Lately, a lot of the things I've done wrong have been on my mind and made me think about why I'm doing these things. I think it's because my father or the man I thought was my father, was so distant."

"Joy, what things are you talking about? You had your father in your life."

"He wasn't my father and he acted like it. I need to know what you know about my real father or for you to tell me who does because I'm no longer believe you don't know anything."

"I told you I didn't..." Curtis voice trailed off when he noticed the look on Joy's face. Her eyes stared at him with such intensity, he wondered if looks could kill, would he be dead now?

"You have to know something." Joy pleaded with him.

"I'm sorry."

Curtis couldn't even look her in the eye. Joy knew it was up to her. Finding her father occurred to her when she was deep in thought about her life and all the things she'd done. Joy felt hatred for the man standing in front of her. She knew that she couldn't believe or trust him. Thinking this caused a chain of thoughts to cruise through her mind. He could even be lying about having sex with her mother before.

"Why don't you lay down on the sofa for a little bit? I'll get you a pillow and a blanket."

"Okay." Joy replied but she didn't want to lie down. She wanted answers.

Curtis returned with the pillow and blanket and set the sofa up. Joy lied down and he went into his bedroom. Feeling wired Joy thought she wouldn't be able to sleep but as soon as she turned on her side and got comfortable, she was out.

38

Joy woke up hours later with a headache. She slept so hard her eyes hurt. She placed both her feet on the floor, and sat back against the sofa. She needed to get her self together. She had money and she had yet to spend it on herself. She grabbed her bag she had under her pillow and opened it, in search of her cell phone. It was four o'clock in the afternoon.

It was really quiet and Joy wondered where Curtis was. She went to his bedroom and knocked on the door. The bathroom had to be in the bedroom because it wasn't one out there, just the living room and kitchen. After no answer, Joy opened the door and she went in.

The room was empty, Curtis was nowhere to be found. Joy went into the bathroom. She patted down her hair. She grabbed a towel from the shelf in the corner and placed in on top of the toilet seat. She didn't have any clean clothes because she'd left her clothes in Dre's car. Thinking of buying new clothes made her smile as she tested the water for her shower.

After her shower, she wrapped herself in the towel. She went to the sink, grabbed the mouthwash. She leaned her head back and swished some in her mouth, spit in the sink and left the bathroom. She sat down on Curtis neatly made bed. She hadn't thought about her mother in a while but suddenly her image appeared in her mind. Joy studied her Mother's features, trying to compare them to hers. Nothing stood out. They didn't look alike at all. She didn't know whether to believe Curtis because she looked nothing like him either. Sadness fell over her. Maybe her life would have been different. She thought that her life was missing only money. Now she knew what people meant when they said, "Money doesn't buy happiness." She had money. She could do what she wanted for a while but she felt like there was a hole in her heart. The thought of spending the money excited her. But then what?

"Fuck this feeling sorry for myself shit." Joy said aloud and got up; the towel came from her around her fell to the floor. She went towards the bathroom to put her clothes back on when she heard a noise behind her, it sounded like a sharp intake of breath. She turned her head to the side. Curtis was standing in the doorway, his eyes glued to Joy's heart shaped ass. Joy stood there longer than she realized before she continued in the bathroom. She hurried into the bathroom picked her clothes off the floor. She put them on as fast as she could.

She opened the door. Curtis was sitting on the bed with his head down. He said nothing when Joy walked by him and went into the living room. She didn't know where to go. She made sure she had everything with her and prepared to leave. Cutis still hadn't come out of the bedroom.

CHAPTER 7

Detective Hartford and Detective Banks finished talking to the manager and the clerk working at the gas station. They still were no closer to identifying the girl on the videotape.

"What did the manager say?" Detective Hartford asked.

"He said the girl came in, beat up and crying. He called the police while she hid behind the counter from Andre Hobbs, until the police arrived. He looked away and when he turned around she was gone. He didn't give a good description, only thing he was sure of, was that she was African American." Detective Banks replied.

"The video tape shows her come in. The tape is dark. She steps through the door but immediately looks to her left. The image of her face isn't clear. The clerk I talked to said he didn't see her come out the back, even though he was back there taking a smoke break."

"We know that the girl was hurt and trying to get away based on the manager's statement. But why did she leave?"

"I say case closed. Hobbs had a .357. The manager and the police both confirmed that much." Detective Banks said, shrugging his shoulders.

"Something in my gut is telling me that it's more to it. We found suitcases in the trunk with clothes belonging to what I guess is both Hobbs and the girl."

"Maybe they had a fight or something."

"Yea, maybe." Detective Hartford wasn't convinced but there were other cases that needed his attention.

Joy was at a complete lost as of what to do. She felt uneasy about being in Philly. Her stomach growled and she realized that she couldn't remember the last time she ate anything. She saw a Wa-wa at the corner and walked faster in its direction.

She decided on a turkey and cheese hoagie. She grabbed a Pepsi from the cooler. There was a line at the counter, so Joy looked around for something else she wanted, hoping the line would die down. By the time Joy got in the line that was down to two people, she had a bag of sun chips and some blue shark candy.

After paying for her food, she walked out the store. She ate as she walked down the street. She needed a place to stash the money; she didn't want to walk around with while she figured out to do.

She passed some houses, so she decided to sit down on one of the steps. She finished her food and tried to plan her next move. She took a few sips of her soda. Her mouth felt watery. She tried to swallow but the feeling only became worst. She drunk some more of her soda. Before she could swallow, she felt her food come back up. Leaning over, she threw up right there on the sidewalk. She dropped her soda and wiped her mouth with the back of her hand. She forgot to grab some napkins and wiped her hand on the leg of her jeans.

Panic began to set in. She thought back to when she last had her period. She had her period since moving to Philly over six months ago. So if she was pregnant, it's not Josh's. Shawn had a vasectomy. Depending on how far along she was, it was down to Dre or Kevin.

She got up from the steps, her stomach still a little queasy. She swallowed, trying to ease the lump in her throat. The urge to break down and cry was strong. She tried to stop the tears from falling. Her eyes watered and she knew once the first tear fell, it was over. She needed to find a doctor to go to. *What the fuck am I gonna do?*

Joy hadn't been to the doctor since moving and she had no clue as to where to go. She looked around at the people walking. She figured she could ask some. The thought came to her that she could look in the phone book.

She walked down the block. Her mind was numb. She continued to walk with no distinct destination. "I could go back to Curtis' apartment to see if he has a phonebook," she thought.

Before Joy realized she was still looking down, she almost brushed into a woman with a stroller at the corner, waiting to cross the street. "Sorry," Joy said and started to walk around her. "It's okay," the woman said with an attitude.

Joy didn't want to ask but she needed to know, "I don't mean to be in your business but can I ask where you went to the doctor when you were pregnant?"

"Why you wanna know?"

"I was just asking because I might be pregnant and I don't know where to go." Joy said, trying to hold her anger in check.

"The closest place I know around here is the clinic on Cottman and Bustleton. If they can't help you there then they can tell you where else to go."

"Thanks." Joy said and walked away.

Joy felt a heavy burden. She couldn't believe that she was pregnant. She didn't need a test to find out. Once she didn't use a condom the first time, it was easier not to after that. Tears rolled down her face. She couldn't control it and she didn't care that people were staring at her as she walked down the street.

She opened her cell phone. The screen was blank. She tried the on button, but nothing happened. She remembered that she didn't charge her phone. She needed to find a way to the clinic. She should have asked the woman how to get there.

Joy wiped her eyes with the back of her hands. She stopped walking and looked around. She saw a bus stop across the street. She crossed the street and crossed again to the side where the bus stop was. A man dressed in a suit and an older lady waited.

Joy stood next to the lady. "Excuse me, can you tell me how to get to Cottman and Bustleton avenue?"

"Yes. You can either walk three blocks that way. Or you can wait here for the fifty-eight. It would take you there."

Joy looked in the direction that the lady pointed and decided to walk. "Thank you."

It didn't take long. She made it to the corner and waited at the light. Directly across the street, she saw a gas station and farther down there was the clinic. The light changed and she crossed. She went to the door and went in the building. She walked over to the desk.

"Can I help you?"

"Umm I need to take a pregnancy test," Joy whispered.

"We only give testing on Wednesday's."

"Okay. Do I need an appointment?"

"No. You just need to come between 12 and 3."

"Okay." Disappointed, she left.

Joy walked outside and looked around. Wednesday was almost three days away and

Joy didn't want to wait that long. She stood there for a minute trying to decide what to do.

She didn't realize that she was standing in front of the door, when she heard a voice behind her.

"Excuse me."

Joy turned around and saw a girl on the other side of the door trying to get out. She moved over so the girl could get out.

The girl looked at Joy and started to walk away but turned around to face Joy.

"I don't mean to be in your business but I heard the receptionist tell you to come back for a pregnancy test. You could go across the street to the Rite Aid and get a home pregnancy test." she said.

Joy looked across the street at the many stores. She had no idea in what direction was talking about.

"Where?" Joy replied after a minute.

"Right over there. Do you see where the Wendy's? It's on that side. You have to walk to the stores in the back of the parking lot."

Joy looked in that direction. From where she was standing she couldn't see it but at least she knew which way to go now.

"Thank you." Joy said walking away from the girl who was still standing there.

"Do you want me to walk with you?" the girl asked.

Joy stopped, "No. It's okay."

"You sure it's not a problem. I mean I know that you don't know me but you don't have to be alone."

Joy thought about it for a minute. She didn't want to go through this alone. She had no one else but this stranger.

"Okay."

CHAPTER 8

In silence, they walked side by side for a minute. Joy was nervous and lost in her own thoughts. She couldn't believe that she might be pregnant. She prayed that the stress of the past few months was the reason for her period's a no show.

"What's your name?" the girl asked breaking Joy from her thoughts.

"Joy."

"I liked that name. I'm Simone."

Finally, they reached the Rite Aid. Simone went in first holding the door for Joy.

Joy followed her to the back. She watched as Simone took charge. She led Joy to the aisle that housed the locked container that held the pregnancy test. She looked up and down the rows until she found the one she was looking for.

"Stay here." was all she said and walked away.

She returned a minute later with the girl from the pharmacy. She showed the girl which one she wanted and both Joy and her followed her to the pharmacy counter.

Joy reached in her bag and slipped out a twenty. She held it out to Simone who looked down at it but didn't take it. Instead, she reached in her own pocket and pulled out the money to pay. She grabbed the bag and started walking back to the front of the store. Joy stood there, confused at the exchange. She held her money in her hand and composed herself, stuffing the money in her jeans pocket; she followed Simone to the front of the store. She caught up to her before Simone noticed she wasn't there.

Simone continued to lead with Joy following behind her. She continued to walk until she reached DEB's clothing store, where she worked. She went behind the counter, spoke to the girls behind there and motioned for Joy. They continued through a door and into a break room with a table, chairs and a refrigerator. A door was in the back of the room.

"That's the bathroom right there."

Joy opened the door without saying a word. The bathroom was tiny but clean. Joy checked the seat before sitting down. She took the test out the bag. She sat there a moment. Tears welled up in her eyes and she wished things to go back to the weekend with her and Kevin and stay in that time.

She took a deep breath and took the test out the box. She looked at the diagram to see what to look for. It would say pregnant if she was and not pregnant if she wasn't.

Simone sat at the table waiting for Joy to come out of the bathroom. When she saw her outside of the clinic, she remembered when she was in the same position. Three years ago when she was just 16, she found out she was pregnant. She felt alone and didn't know her options. Once she told her mother that her stepbrother was the father of the baby, her mother threw both of them out the house. Her stepbrother who was two years younger moved to California with his mother and wanted nothing to do with her or "it", he told her while packing his bags. She wanted an abortion but needed parental consent. At the clinic, after talking to one of the counselors she decided to put the baby up for adoption. Now her daughter was somewhere out there hopefully in a better home than she was raised in.

Lost in thought, she barely heard Joy come out the bathroom. She looked up and could tell by the look on Joy's face that it wasn't good news.

Joy's chest heaved up and down as she tried to catch her breath. Tears streamed down her face and she stumbled to a chair and she put her head in her hands and broke down. Simone watched her for a moment before she moved her chair closer.

"Joy, It's going to be okay. Is there anyone you want me to call for you?"

"No. I have nobody."

"Okay. I know we don't know each other that well but I'm here for you. It wasn't too long ago I was in your shoes."

Joy looked into Simone's eyes and saw how sincere she seemed but something in her reminded her to be cautious.

"I can't believe this happened to me."

"What about the father?"

Joy thought about it. "I guess it depends on how far along I am."

CHAPTER 9

Joy thanked Simone and was on her way in a direction unknown, when she heard someone running behind her, calling her name. She turned to see Simone and stopped.

"Here's my number, in case you need something," Simone said and pressed a piece of paper in Joy's hand.

Joy took the number and continued to walk towards Roosevelt Boulevard. She tried to think anything that would help her. She thought about who could be the father of her baby. Shawn had a vasectomy. She wasn't sure about Dre because they just started having sex and she didn't have her period in months. "So it has to be Kevin." Joy yelled in excitement.

She saw a cab in at a Dunkin Donuts drive thru window and she ran to catch it. The driver waiting noticed her running towards him and rolled down the window.

"Where you headed?"

She gave him the directions to Kevin's apartment as she got in. The back of the cab smelled like feet and cabbage. Joy rolled the window down and stuck her face outside the cab. She rolled with her face out the whole way there. When the driver pulled up to Kevin's, she paid him, and got out.

Ten minutes later, the cab had pulled off and she was still standing at the bottom of the stairs that led to Kevin's apartment door. Her hand shook in midair as she reached for the banister. She was afraid of being rejected.

Tired of standing, she sat down on the bottom two steps. She thought about what she would say and nothing seemed right. She didn't know how long she had sat before she forced herself to chalk up her fear and walked up the stairs. When she reached out to knock on the door, it flew open.

Kevin stood there with his keys in his hand, a shocked expression on his face. Joy could see the anger and the pain in his eyes.

"Joy." he said, staring at her.

She stood speechless and her heart grew tight in her chest. It wasn't because it hurt her to see the man she loved almost from sight after months away from him. It was because directly behind him was his new bitch.

"You okay daddy?" the bitch asked, looking directly at Joy.

Kevin remained silent and stared at Joy.

"Tanya?"

"What are you doing here?" Tanya asked stepping around Kevin.

Joy looked from Tanya to Kevin, who looked down at his feet still not saying a word.

"What do you want with my man?" Tanya asked, getting in Joy's face.

"Oh so now he's your man now?" Joy thought to beat Tanya's face in but Tanya's belly stuck out through her t-shirt.

"Yeah ho."

Joy smirked at Tanya. "Who you calling a ho. You're the one with multiple baby fathers. None of your kids even stay with you. The baby you're carrying now makes what; 7 kids, 7 fathers?

"And another thing, can you say that you're having his baby?" Joy said and rubbed her still flat stomach. Tanya's scrunched up her face, like she tasted something sour.

"You're pregnant?" Kevin asked.

"You sure it's not some other nigga's baby you carrying bitch?"

"I'm sure. I haven't had sex with anyone else, so I know who my baby daddy is unlike you, bitch." Joy lied, hoping that it was Kevin's baby.

Kevin's face showed his disbelief. He stepped closer to Joy. "Really?"

Tanya sucked her teeth and pushed Kevin aside as she got back in Joy's face. Joy smiled. Tanya punched her in the face, catching her on the side of her right eye. Something in Joy snapped. You couldn't tell that she never been in a fight before. She grabbed Tanya by her hair, bringing her head low, as she kneed her in the face. She heard a crunch and knew she broke something. Tanya fell to the ground and Joy let her go.

Kevin reached down and helped Tanya to her feet. Her face was covered with blood and her nose was crooked. It looked like it was broken. Kevin winced when he looked at her. He leaned her against the wall. She wept, holding her nose and staring at Joy like she wanted to kill her while she kept her distance.

Tears rolled down Joy's face. It wasn't because of pain; the punch Tanya threw stung her face and swelled the right side of her face. It was because she was angry at Tanya for being with Kevin and then having the nerve to put her hands on her.

"I should take you two to the hospital to make sure everything was alright with yall and the babies are okay." Kevin shook his head and grabbed Tanya's arm. He led her down the steps and to the car. Joy followed behind them. At the car he opened the back door for Tanya to get in. She looked at him like he was crazy but got in. Joy opened the door and slid in the passenger seat with a smile on her face.

CHAPTER 10

"Can I help you?" the guard at the desk at Einstein Hospital asked.

"Yes. These two need to be looked at. They were in a fight and umm they both pregnant." Kevin said really fast.

The guard looked at him as if he wanted to say something but didn't.

"Both babies aren't mine, so you can stop looking at me like that." he clarified

"Okay." the guard said holding both hands out in front of him. "Jeff, can you bring another wheelchair," he said into his walkie-talkie.

Another guard came form the double doors on the side with a wheelchair, placing it beside the one already there. He motioned for Tanya and Joy to have a seat. Kevin pushed Joy and Jeff pushed Tanya. The first room they came to Joy was rolled in. The one next to it was Tanya's. A nurse came in and told them both to get undress and put on the gowns that were on top of the bed.

"Do you want me to step out?" Kevin asked Joy.

"You done seen it all before. But you might as well go in there with your girlfriend." she said, dryly.

"She's not my girlfriend. She...."

"Yeah? She was at you're apartment, calling you daddy n shit." Joy said cutting him off.

"It's not what you think."

"What is it then? You know what I don't care. Where is the damn doctor?"

Tears rolled down her face. She heard the doctor next door talking to Tanya. Thinking about Tanya and Kevin together made Joy angrier. She wiped her face with but her face became soaked again half a second later. The nurse came in, handed her a cup. "I need a urine sample. The bathroom's on the corner." she said and left back out.

Joy swung her legs over the side of the bed and stood up. She grabbed the sheet off the bed and wrapped it around herself. She walked pass Kevin without saying anything.

When she finished in the bathroom, she went back into the room. Kevin was gone. Joy stuck her head back outside of the curtain and looked left then right, nothing. She went back to the bed to lay down. She placed her hand on her stomach. A funny feeling spread across her stomach and she felt something move. She had denied the feeling in the past but now she knew that it was a baby.

The nurse came in and drew three tubes of blood. She then placed an IV in Joy's arm. "These are fluids so you don't get dehydrated," she stated before she left.

She couldn't believe how different everything was. As the months went by she lost more and more of herself and she didn't even know who she was anymore. The tears started again, just as Kevin came back in. He held a bottle of Pepsi and a cup of ice.

He held the cup out to her, "It's only ice. The nurse said that was all you could have."

Joy took the cup and sat it down on the table. She rolled on her side, turning her back on him.

"Look, Tanya just showed up at my door, right before you came. She was crying begging me to take her to the train station. She said that she was staying with her man at his apartment. She said she had no place to go but back to New York because her man left one day and never came back. She stayed in his apartment until the manager threw her out."

Joy knew that Tanya was talking about Rob. "You expect me to believe that?" She said still trying to play hard; she knew Kevin was telling the truth.

"She told me what happened with Shawn. I almost believed you for a second about the baby and not being with no one else but from the way you acting I know that shit's true." he stared at her with his face twisted up in disgust.

"Kevin, it's not what you think." she heard herself say and winced. She sounded like he did a minute ago.

"I don't know what she told you but what I said is true."

"Joy if this is my baby I want to be with you. I'm tired of the games. I want a family and I hope that's what you want. I can't keep dealing with this shit from you. I must be a crazy nigga for wanting to have anything to do with your ass. You ruined my life but I still have love in my heart for you."

Before Joy could respond, the doctor came in.

"Hi Miss Williams. I'm the Resident OB-GYN here tonight. My name is Dr. Cook. We tested your blood and urine and they both showed that you are pregnant. Can you tell me how far along you are?"

"I'm not sure.' Joy said nervously and looked at Kevin.

"When was the date of the first day of your last menstrual cycle?"

"I can't remember. I had a lot going on." Joy said embarrassed.

"Okay. So I take it you have not had prenatal care."

"No."

"We will perform a vaginal exam on you and then I'll do an ultrasound to make sure the baby is okay."

"Okay."

On cue the nurse wheeled in the cart with the supplies. Joy looked at. There were gloves, large q-tips, some other sticks with looked like wire on the end, some packets that said surgical lubricant on them and a large plastic object that looked sort of like a shoe horn.

The doctor made small talk, trying to get Joy to relax. She explained the reason for everything she used. She handed everything to the nurse who would send it to the lab. When the nurse came back she pushed a machine in. It looked like a computer with different color buttons.

Dr. Cook plugged the machine in and turned it on. She then lifted up Joy's gown, exposing Joy's stomach and put some petroleum jelly on stomach. Kevin who stepped out the room to give the doctor room to examine Joy came back in. Joy was excited. They watched as the doctor rubbed what looked like a funny shaped mouse on Joy's stomach.

At first she moved in side to side. They stared at the screen. When she found the baby she stopped and pressed a harder in that area. She stared for a while.

"This is your baby's arm and here is a leg. Wow, this little one is moving like crazy."

The doctor pressed some buttons and lines came on the screen. She measured the baby's head and body. Okay, judging from the size of your baby, I will say that you are about 11 weeks and 3 days. Your due date is December 4."

Looking at the screen, Joy couldn't believe that she was looking at her baby. She couldn't even think of the words to describe the feeling she had. She never felt this way before, a true and deep happiness. "Eleven weeks is about right for it to be Kevin's," Joy thought and looked at Kevin. He had tears in his eyes.

"Do you know what it is?" Kevin asked.

"It's still to early to tell. In a few more weeks you will be able to find out."

"It looks like a boy." Kevin said.

"Okay baby look at mommy and smile." the doctor said to the screen. Joy laughed at this and studied the screen. She couldn't make too much out. When the doctor was finished, she wiped Joy's stomach off and pulled her gown down. She reached on the side of the machine and tore off the paper on the side. Joy could see they were sonogram pictures. She handed Joy the last two. She kept the rest, told Joy she would be back to talk to her after she checked her test results.

They only had to wait five more minutes until the doctor returned. She said that everything was okay with the baby and with Joy. She ordered her to take it easy and to get prenatal care right away. She gave Joy a prescription for prenatal vitamins and said it was okay for them to leave.

Now inside the car, it was nothing but silence. Joy let out a loud breath. She should be happy that her baby was okay. The problem in the backseat overshadow that Joy turned around and looked at Tanya, who was crying.

Her entire nose was bandaged and her face was swollen.

"Would you shut the fuck up?"

"You broke my nose in three places. You lucky I didn't press charges."

"No bitch. You lucky." Joy threatened.

Tanya saw something in Joy's eyes she never noticed before and backed down. She slumped back and continued to whimper.

Joy turned back around and glared at Kevin. He looked straight ahead at the road. After spending five hours in the ER, Joy was exhausted. She wanted to leave Tanya there, looking pitiful, but Kevin insisted that they take her with them.

Finally, they reached Kevin's apartment. When Tanya went to get out the car, Joy stopped her.

"Wait right here."

She took Kevin's keys and went inside his apartment. She returned with the bag that she guessed were Tanya's things from out of Kevin's living room.

"You just going to let her do this to me?" Tanya asked Kevin.

"You ask me to take you to the bus station, that's what I'm going do." he said, following Joy's lead.

CHAPTER 11

After they got rid of Tanya, Joy thought her Kevin would be nothing but happier. Watching Tanya get on the bus was the last time she actually felt any kind of Joy. Three weeks had passed by and all she wanted to do was lay around and eat. She wasn't showing but she had a slight bulge to her belly.

She couldn't stand the sight of Kevin. Everything he did bothered her all of the sudden. She found herself putting the cap on the toothpaste after him, putting the items back he used to make a sandwich. If he breathed too hard while he slept, she would wake up and then couldn't go back to sleep.

She chalked it up to them spending too much time together. She still had the money in her bag and she carried around where ever she went, even to the bathroom. When Kevin commented on it she just told him that she took the bag just in case she needed something and she knew that she wouldn't feel like getting up. He left her alone, calling her lazy.

When she got back to Kevin's the night after the incident with Tanya, she had looked for a hiding place but she wasn't sure if it would go unfound. She wanted to spend it and at least buy some new clothes. She hadn't left the apartment in three weeks and stayed naked.

She constantly fought Kevin off because he took her nakedness as her invitation that she wanted sex. She couldn't stand having sex with him anymore. That didn't stop Kevin from trying to get her in the mood.

"Kevin I don't feel like." Joy whined as Kevin kissed her neck.

"Can you at least suck it, something?" he took her hand and pressed it on his rock hard dick.

"No." she said, and turned her back on him.

"Joy. It's been a minute. You don't even care. Other pregnant women don't have a problem having sex with their man."

"What the fuck does that mean?" she yelled, turned back around to face him.

"It means what I said."

"You better not be throwing that bitch Tanya in my face. She's a ho so I know she let you hit."

"What? Joy you on some shit. You better not be smoking nothing with my kid in you."

"Whatever." she mumbled and turned her back on him again.

Kevin moved over, closer to Joy so that his dick rubbed up against her behind.

"Stop Kevin." She yelled, trying to move away from him but she was already as close to the edge as she could get.

Kevin put his arms around her waist and moved up, rubbing her breast. Joy laid still. He took that as a sign that she was either sleep or she would let him get some. He reached down and lifted her leg up some, so he could slide in. Out of nowhere Joy elbowed him in the stomach.

"Shit. You know what..." Kevin didn't finish his sentence. He grabbed Joy by her hair and pulled her to the middle of the bed.

"Owwww Kevin. The baby."

"The baby will be find, just be still."

Holding down her arms with one hand, he guided his dick inside her. He couldn't believe how warm and wet she was. "It's true what they say about pregnant women," he thought, gritting his teeth. He looked down into Joy's face. She frowned and her eyes were closed real tight. He stopped, "Joy, I'm not hurting you am I?" he let go of her arms and started kissing her face. His lips were wet from her tears. He felt ashamed about what he did to her so he climbed off her and laid next to her.

"Joy let me hold you. And don't elbow me."

She turned her back but allowed him to hold her. Her body was stiff and he could tell that she didn't want him touching her. He let her go and rolled onto his side of the bed. He would lay there for ten minutes. His dick was still hard. He looked over to see if Joy was awake, maybe he could change her mind. But she was knocked out, snoring. Kevin sucked his teeth and climbed out of bed. He threw on the clothes that he stepped out of and left on the floor.

He glanced at Joy on the way out of the bedroom. He grabbed his cars keys and left, slamming the door behind him.

CHAPTER 12

Joy had no idea how long she was asleep but when she woke up at six in the morning, Kevin was gone. At first Joy was happy to have the bed alone so she could stretch out. When she tried closing her eyes, she started imaging all the things Kevin could be doing with some bitch.

She tossed and turned for a half and hour before she dozed off again. When she woke up again two hours later, Kevin was still gone. This time Joy began to worry. She reached for her cell phone to call him. It ranged once and then his voicemail came on.

"Shit. This nigga better not be fucking a other chick." Joy thought.

She walked out the living room, headed towards the kitchen, intending to get something to eat. She went to the front door and looked out. Kevin's car was sitting in the usual spot. Kevin was in the driver seat, which was pushed all the way back in the backseat. He was sleep on his back with his arm over his face. Joy sucked her teeth and closed the door.

She went back in the kitchen. She opened the refrigerator and took out some eggs, milk and the butter. Recently, Kevin taught her how to scrambled eggs. It became her favorite thing to eat because it was the only thing she could make. She looked in the cabinet for the black pepper and the seasoned salt.

After making a sandwich with the eggs, Joy went back into the bedroom to eat. Before she even made it to the bed, half of the sandwich was gone.

"Damn, I should have made two." she said aloud after stuffing the last bite in her mouth.

She sat for a while flipping channels. After only a few minutes, she got up. She couldn't stand being in the apartment any longer. The money was burning a hole in her pocket. She was so anxious to spend it that she counted it every chance she got. When she was bored, she made lists of the things she wanted to do with the money and of the things she wanted to buy.

She threw on the only outfit she had. She had no friends, still she scrolled through her phone list. Most of the numbers were all the local fast food restaurants. She came across Josh's number. The look on his face the moment he realized that Joy shot him flashed through her mind. She shook her head as if to shake the image out her mind. She erased the number and continued down the list. She came across the cab company. She called them to see if they had a cab available. They did, she waited the ten minutes that the operator quoted.

After making like three previous trips to the bathroom, Joy was frustrated. She was flushing the toilet when she thought she heard a car horn. She listened but didn't hear anything. She washed her hands and when she got back to the bathroom, she picked her phone up off the bed. She noticed that she had two missed calls. She scrolled down the list. Both calls were from the same number that Joy didn't recognized. She walked to the front door and looked out. Kevin's car was gone. Joy sucked her teeth and closed the door.

Joy called the cab company. The operator told her that she dispatched a cab to her that arrived about ten minutes ago. A man outside the residence told him that the cab wasn't needed any longer. The cab driver called her to confirm and received no answer, so he left.

Frustrated, Joy hung up on the operator and called Kevin. When he answered, Joy yelled, "Why the fuck did you send my cab away."

"First of all, who you talking to like that? Second, where you get money for a cab? You going to see that nigga."

"No."

"Then where you was going? Like I said, you are going to see that fucking nigga. If you leave the house, you better not come back."

"Kevin it's not like that. I'm not going to see him. I can't anyway."

"What you mean you can't? What he threw you away after he used you up. Is that why you came back to me? I mean you act like you can't stand me and you won't even let me touch."

" But Kevin." Joy whined and began to cry, the only way she knew to get sympathy.

"You know what Joy. We'll talk about this later, when I get home."

"Kevin, how long you going to be?"

"Don't worry bout it. You just better be there when I get back."

"Kevin I just wanted to get out the house."

"I'll take you out when I get back."

"Where are you?"

"I'm at my brother's house, I'll be there in a little bit." Kevin's hung up.

Joy was at a loss as to what she should do. She didn't like how Kevin was acting. She did feel bad at how she was treating him. It was the pregnancy. She tried to tell him that.

Being pregnant with Kevin's child, Joy knew that he wouldn't throw her out for real. Though she was always tired, cranky, and constantly complaining Kevin never got mad or irritated with her. His problem was that he was trying to control her. She looked in the phone book for a different cab company. Once she called them, she went outside to wait.

She held her bag close. She only had about three thousand on her. The remainder of the money, she placed in Ziploc bags and taped them on the box spring under the bed. She hoped that she made the right decision by leaving it there. In the back of her mind, she knew that Kevin could throw her out and she wouldn't be able to get to it.

The cab driver pulled up and honked the horn to get Joy's attention. Joy was so caught in her thoughts that she didn't notice the cab pull up. She inched up, "Damn, my belly ain't even big yet and I'm having trouble getting up." she said to herself as she walked down the stairs. Her hand was on the door handle of the cab when Kevin pulled up. They clashed eyes and Joy hesitated.

"Come on. Are you getting in?" the cab driver yelled out his window.

"Ummm, yeah," Joy opened the door. By then Kevin was right behind her.

"Joy where the fuck you going?" he said, pulling her away from the door.

"Come on buddy leave her alone."

"You shut the fuck up. Joy, go back in the house."

Joy stood there a few seconds longer before she sucked her teeth, closed the door and went up to the apartment steps.

She heard Kevin ask, "Where were you taking her?"

The cab driver replied, "Some mall in the northeast."

"Aight," he said and walked away.

Joy was at the top of the stairs watching Kevin. When she saw him walking towards her she went in the house. Kevin came in the bedroom, Joy was sitting on the bed, looking down at the floor.

"Joy, why were you going to the mall? You were going to meet that nigga, wasn't you?"

"No."

"Don't lie to me." Kevin yelled causing Joy to jump. She looked at him and began to shake. She never saw him so upset. Not even when he was locked up after the big fight between him and Josh's cousin.

"Kevin, I'm not... " Before she could finish her sentence Kevin grabbed her by the hair and pulled her back on the bed. He was standing over her with his face pressed to hers.

"Joy, don't lie. Is that my baby you're carrying?"

"Yes."

"After you have this baby and were getting a DNA test. If it's not mine I want you to forget you know me."

"Kevin." Joy was crying so hard that she hard trouble catching her breath.

"Kevin I can't breathe. You have to take me to the hospital."

"Shit Joy, stop playing. Now you're being a drama queen."

"I'm not playing." Kevin looked at Joy and noticed her face was flushed. Kevin picked her up and carried her to the car. He put her on the ground while he opened the door and helped her get in. He watched her and saw that her chest was rapidly moving up and down. He got in beside her.

"Joy I'm so sorry. This is my fault, I just get so mad. You know I went threw this before with my ex."

Joy didn't comment. She was busy worrying about what she was going to do. She was trying to calm down. Since she stopped crying her breathing was returning to normal. She wasn't going to say nothing to Kevin. He still was apologizing.

"Kevin I think I'm okay now."

"You sure?" He was relieved he didn't get mad. He made a quick u-turn and headed back to his apartment.

CHAPTER 13

Joy was tired of having to deal with Kevin's controlling ways. He was jealous of a dead man. He didn't know that Shawn was dead. Every time Kevin would bring him up, Joy just wanted scream and just tell Kevin that he was dead. He was driving her crazy. She questioned whether it was a good idea to come back here. The only time she left the apartment now was to go to her doctor appointments.

Now that she was almost six mouths pregnant, she was getting more worried by the minute. All she could think about was the baby not being Kevin's. He might murder her or something, having been through it before, she thought constantly. Joy found it hard to watch how excited Kevin had become. He talked about the baby all of the time. To make it worst, he now knew it was a girl. When the doctor gave them the news, Kevin cried in the office.

Joy only knew one way to deal with her problems, runaway from them. That's what she planned to do. She hadn't seen or heard from Simone since the day she found out she was pregnant, but she hoped that she would come through for her again just like she did that day. She was her only option. She didn't know anyone else.

She found the piece of paper that Simone wrote her number on and dialed the number. After the fifth ring, Joy realized that she didn't think about what she would do if Simone didn't answer or had new number, it has been a few months now.

Just as she took the phone from her ear, she heard someone shout hello.

"Hey, It's Joy." she said, and waited to see if Simone remembered her.

"Oh, Ohhhh hey. It's been a while. How have you been?"

"Okay, I guess."

"Are you sure you sound sad or something?"

Joy told Simone everything that happen from when she left Simone's job until now.

"Damn, that sounds crazy." Simone said, when Joy was done.

"Yea, so I need a place to stay to get my head right."

"Well..." Simone hesitated.

"I only wanted to know if you knew where I could just pay cash for an apartment and not have to worry about paperwork or anything." Joy said, irritated.

"Oh yea. You can probably get something in the building where I live. My boo is cool with the manager. You probably have to shoot the manager a couple dollars.

"Ok. That's no problem. Give me the directions and I'll be on my way."

Joy was relived to hear the good news. She hated to leave without telling Kevin but he just was too controlling. She made sure she collected all the money from under the bed. She did leave him one of the plastic bags with money in it. She didn't count it, she didn't know how much it was but she knew it was several stacks. She left a sticky note next to it that read, *I love you, Joy*.

As she got in the cab, she glanced back because she expected Kevin to come home and stop her. She knew that he wouldn't because he had a wedding in Edgewater, NJ. In fifteen minutes she arrived at Simone's. Simone lived in the Northeast, right around the corner from her job.

The building looked a rundown. Weeds grew out of the bricks and the grass was overgrown. Joy walked through the front door and went to the intercom. She buzzed Simone's apartment and waited. Seconds later she was on the elevator. Once she got to the door, she listened. She heard a males voice but couldn't make out what he was saying. So she knocked. A short man about 5'2 answered the door, a toothpick stuck out his mouth. He sucked on the toothpick, as he looked Joy up and down. Joy blew her breath loud to show him her irritation but he didn't notice. He was one step up from being ugly. He had no type of body. He was stick skinny, with a huge gut. Joy had had about enough of him, when she heard Simone tell him to move and let her in. Joy thought that they made a funny looking couple. Simone was 5"7'. She had long, wavy, jet-black hair. She had flawless golden brown skin. She was very pretty and her body was top notch. She had a tiny fame but a fat ass with melon size breast.

"Have a seat Joy." Joy sat down at a table that was in the living room.

"Jamek, this is Joy. Joy this is Jamek."

"Was sup?"

"Hey." Joy said.

Instantly, Joy disliked Jamek. He talked too loud and his only goal at thirty-two was to be a rapper. He made this known to Joy right away. Just in case she knew someone or someway he could get a deal with. After fifteen minutes of Jamek talking nonstop, Simone was even tired of him.

"Jamek didn't you say you had something to do?"

"Oh yeah. I'm out. Joy holler at me. Simone got the number," he said then left.

"Damn, I'm glad that nigga gone." Simone said and laughed.

"Was that *your* boo?" Joy asked trying to keep from laughing.

"Girl, hell no! That's just the weed man. He always looks out when I cop from him. He double on anything I buy. Even if I get just a nick, he hand me a dime bag.

"You smoke?"

"Not in a minute."

"Oh shit, yeah I forgot." Simone said, reaching over to run Joy's belly. Joy showed fully now thru her oversized tee shirt. As she looked down at her sweatpants she thought about the day Kevin came home with them. She asked him can he take her to get some maternity clothes and he came home with bags of sweatpants and tee shirts.

"I can't wait until I have this baby."

"Do you know what you're having?"

"A girl. Can I use your bathroom?"

"Yeah. Go in the bedroom, it's in the corner."

Joy got up, letting out a breath. It was harder and harder to get up everyday. She waddled to the bathroom. When she came out the bathroom, she saw that someone else was sitting at the table with their back turned towards Joy. She walked back to her seat and sat back down. She made eye contact with the person and knew right away that it was a female. Despite the baggy clothes and the fitted hat, She had a pretty face, with small facial features and gray and hazel eyes.

When Joy realized that she been studying her, she turned away. Simone stopped talking and introduced them, "Joy, *this* is my boo Ronnie."

"Hi." Ronnie said in the softest voice Joy had ever heard.

"Hey." Joy said, holding her hand up in a nervous wave.

Simone laughed, she loved the reaction she got from people who didn't know she was gay.

"You got a problem?" Ronnie said taking offense.

"No. I was just surprised."

"Ronnie cut that shit out." Simone said.

"Where you say you met this broad at again?"

Joy's hand went to her stomach. "*Pregnant or not, I will fuck this bitch up.*" She thought.

"Ronnie don't start your shit. Can you just do me this solid? Joy's not gay. Don't you see that she pregnant? Chill."

"Yeah I don't know why you trying to help her. It's a reason behind it."

Joy knew that Ronnie was jealous. Though she remained quiet, she wanted to tell her she had nothing to worry about. She shook her head but she got up and strolled to the door and left. Once she left, Simone tried to laugh off her behavior.

"I'm sorry bout that. I don't know why she acts like that. I think she's bipolar on the low."

"It's cool." Joy said like it didn't bother, but she knew that she would have to watch out for Ronnie.

The wait wasn't long. Ronnie came back with a woman in her forties. She wore glasses but looked at Joy over the lens. "How old are you?"

"22," Joy lied.

"Okay. I'll show you the apartment. You need to have all the money up front, today."

"Okay."

Joy followed the woman out the door. They walked down the hall and turned the corner and came to a door. The manager took out the keys and opened the apartment. She allowed Joy to walk in first. It was smaller than Simone's but had the same setup. There was the living room with the kitchen off to the side. As soon as you walked into the apartment, the bedroom was the door in front of you.

"How much?" Joy asked.

"$710 everything included. Altogether it will be $2130 for first, last and security. Rent is due every month on the first. Pay it directly to me. I'll show you where the office is. If I'm not there, wait until I come."

"Okay."

"Let me show where the office is."

They went down to the first floor and into the office. Joy asked to use the bathroom, where she counted off the money. She took an extra $500 for the lady looking out. Even though she didn't ask, Joy knew that she expected something in return.

She paid the manager and got the keys. She went up to her apartment. She felt as empty as her new apartment.

CHAPTER 14

Joy never thought ahead about anything that she did, so she had no clue what to do next. She stood in the middle of her floor. She didn't own anything to put in her apartment. Months ago, this would have been fun but she realized that she really didn't want to be bothered. She didn't even have a way to get around.

She stood up against the wall. She didn't want to sit on the floor because she knew she would have a hard time getting up. Her cell phone rung but she ignored it. Kevin was looking for her. She knew that he would blow up her phone as soon as he knew that she was gone. It was dark and she already regretted her decision to leave Kevin. She was starving. With Kevin she never had to worry about food. His refrigerator and cabinets were always stocked and he had a drawer full of menus, for any kind of the food she could think of.

The baby kicked as if she agreed with her. Joy rubbed her belly. She still had a lot of doctor appointments to go to. Not only did Kevin take her, he was her support. Deep down, she cared about Kevin. He was always in her thoughts. She prayed to God that the baby she was carrying was his because she wanted to share so much with him. She was too busy thinking about what she wanted for herself. Kevin stood by her and he wasn't even sure that it was his baby. She didn't think before now about what she would do with the baby. She couldn't take care of the baby alone. She didn't know anything about raising a child. She went down the call log in her phone and looked for the number of the cab company she used earlier. She called and had a 45-minute wait. She figured he would forgive her if she cried and apologize enough. She dialed Kevin next. When he didn't answer, she decided to listen to the messages he left.

"Joy where are you and where did you get this money from? Whoever you stole it from better not come looking for me. All your shit seems to fall back on me. You better not be with that nigga. Fucking him with my daughter in you."

"You know something Joy I guessed by now that your are not coming back. It's been hours and I aint heard nothing from your ass. You think you can throw a few dollars and shit cool? When you have the baby, I'm getting a DNA test and then if she's mine I'm getting custody."

"This is my third and last message to you bitch. Fuck you and I don't want nothing to do with you. I don't even know what I'm doing even blowing up your phone. All the shit I've done for you when you had nothing or nobody. You probably out smutting that nigga, you bitch. I know why you wasn't giving me none."

"Damn," Joy thought.

After hearing Kevin's messages, she had second thoughts about going to him. He needs time to cool off. Joy knew that she couldn't stay the night. She didn't have a lamp or a blanket even if she attempted to sleep on the floor.

She didn't know whether she should let Kevin cool down or not. The cab driver called and let her know that he was outside. She walked towards the elevator, Simone and Ronnie were coming out there apartment. Ronnie sucked her teeth.

"Where you headed?" Simone asked.

"Don't really know." Joy said, still undecided about what she was going to do about Kevin.

"Do you need help or anything?" Simone asked as they stepped on the elevator.

"Not really. I just need to get to a store and get some things."

"Oh, it's a whole bunch of stores on Cottman."

"I saw a lot of clothing stores. I need a shower curtain and stuff like that."

"There's a Sears up there. Is that cab for you?" Simone asked when they walked outside.

"Yeah."

"You don't have a waste your money on no cab. I can run you up there."

Simone didn't notice the look Ronnie gave her but Joy did. It made her shake a little. She couldn't understand why she hated her so much. Ronnie lit a cigarette and started blowing smoke in Joy's direction. Joy moved closer to the cab.

"It's cool. I don't want to hold y'all up or nothing, but thanks," Joy said and jumped in the cab. She didn't like the way Ronnie was looking at her.

As the cab pulled away from the curb, Joy knew that she wasn't coming back. She headed to the only person she had left, the person who was there when she had nothing. She only hoped that he would take her back again. She felt like that Jasmine Sullivan song, "I need you bad." She played out what she would do and say to get him to forgive her.

When she arrived at the apartment, Kevin wasn't there. Joy used the key hidden on top of the doorframe to get in. She went straight to the kitchen to get something to eat. When she turned on the light, she saw roses and a card in the trash. She reached in and took them out.

Opening the card, she smiled at the cover that read "Thinking of you." The inside was blank except for what Kevin wrote, "Joy I'm sorry for the way I've been treating you. I love you." Joy read this, tears dropped from her eyes onto the card. She searched for something to put the roses in. She found a pitcher in the cabinet. The longer she stared at the roses and the card, the harder she would cry.

She went into the bedroom when she lost her appetite. She wanted to rest. The money sat on the bed where Joy left it, but Kevin had placed a towel over it. Joy pushed everything over and climbed under the covers. She closed her eyes and cried herself to sleep.

CHAPTER 15

Hunger woke Joy up hours later. Her eyes hurt from all the crying. She went and peed for what felt like two hours. When she came out the bathroom, she noticed that clock read 2am and Kevin was nowhere to be found. Joy got up and looked outside to see if Kevin was sleeping in his car again. No sign of Kevin's car. Joy went back into the kitchen. She put on a pack of Ramen Noodles and ate Cheez-Its until they were ready. After her meal, she debated about calling Kevin and decided against it. Her phone had died anyway and she just placed it on the charger.

She figured he was still mad. She got back in the bed and fell back into a deep sleep. When she awoke again it was 8:30am. Joy was upset that Kevin never came home. "He didn't even know that she was here, so where is he?"

Joy turned on the TV and flipped through channels. She stopped on The CW channel and watched the guy do the weather. She was lost in thought about what she wanted to say to Kevin, when she heard the news lady say something about a massacre at a wedding reception last night. She turned the volume up.

"Police tell us last night in the Northeast section of Philadelphia, a man believed to be in his thirties, crashed a wedding reception, killing seven people. The names of the victims haven't been released. The shooter is still at large and police are asking that anyone with any information please contact them. They want to review the videotape and talk to witnesses before they released a suspect description. We will have more on this later today."

Joy ran in the kitchen and looked for the calendar Kevin kept in the drawer. She looked at yesterday's date and read where Kevin worked. He had an 11am in Springfield, and then 5pm in Byberry. Joy dropped the calendar. There was a sharp ringing in her ears and she felt like she was under water.

She panicked as she searched for her phone. First she checked in the bedroom, she remembered that she had the phone in the kitchen on the charger. The phone was still dead because she forgot to connect the charger to the socket. She plugged it in and each second that it took for it to come on felt like hours. Finally, it came on. The phone beeped, she had a voicemail message and her hands shook as she waited for the message to come on.

"Joy," she heard Kevin's voice and covered her mouth to keep from screaming. Tears flowed from her eyes. He sounded so far away. She heard him cough and he continued. "I love you. I know that you're carrying my little girl. Don't worry..."

Joy heard him gasp a deep breath. "Joy I..." She listened to see if she could hear him but he didn't say anything else. People shouted in the background. She kept the phone pressed to her ear until the message cut off.

After saving the message, she pressed the button to retrieve the time and date. The call came in at 8:03 last night. Joy went back to the bedroom and sat on the bed. She tried to slow her breathing. "No." she screamed. She curled up into a ball in the middle of the bed. "This can't be happening." She said out loud. She tried to think of what she could do. Her mind was blank and her own loud crying blocked out her thoughts.

She jumped up. *Maybe it was a mistake. Kevin is okay; he is just injured and couldn't call yet.* She reached for her phone. She couldn't remember what the number was on the news so she dialed 911. She told the dispatcher that she was trying to find out if her husband was one of the people killed in the shooting. She was transferred to a Philadelphia number. She repeated the same thing to the person who answered the phone.

"Ma'am, what is your name?"

"Joy Jacobs. My husband's name is Kevin Jacobs."

"Okay, hold on one moment please."

Five seconds later, a man picked up the phone. "Mrs. Jacobs? Do you have someone there with you?"

"No."

"Is there anyway you can come down to the station?"

"Um I don't know."

"If you need a ride we can send someone to come get you."

Joy didn't answer. She already knew. Kevin was gone. Her chest hurt. It felt like her heart had shattered. She was on her knees. She clutched the phone, no longer listening to what the man was saying. She closed the phone.

The room felt like it was spinning, Joy closed her eyes. She tried to take a step and before she knew it, she fell to the floor.

CHAPTER 16

Joy opened her eyes to a blinding pain. She looked around and realized that she was on the floor. Her head throbbed and she had no idea how long she was out. She climbed to her feet. A sharp pain shot from her stomach down to her vagina. She felt wetness travel down her leg. "Shit!" she screamed.

She needed to get to the hospital. She didn't want to call an ambulance. She called a cab, but the wait was too long. She had no choice but to call Simone but Simone didn't answer. Ronnie answered and hung up before Joy could say anything. Joy waited for the cab.

Joy sat on the bed bent over, holding her stomach. She felt the baby moving. All she could do was cry. This was too much for her to handle. She laid back and rocked. An hour passed and the pain subsided. She closed her eyes and went to sleep.

When she opened her eyes, a man was staring over her. He frowned at her but he didn't say anything when he realized that she was awake.

"What are you doing here?"

"I'm Mr. Jacobs' landlord. I don't think you're on the lease."

"You're not supposed to be in here...."

"You know what Miss, you have to leave. I heard the awful news. Kevin's uncle called me this morning and said that he would pay me if I packed up all this stuff by the time he came later today."

"So soon?"

"Yep."

"Do you have his uncle's number?"

"No. You have to go. If not I'm going to have to call the police."

Joy lifted herself on her elbows. Her entire body hurt and she didn't want to move. She swung her legs over the side and got out the bed. She was glad that she was still fully dress because the man never took his eyes off her. He watched as she gathered her stuff.

"Can I at least use the bathroom?"

"Go ahead."

As soon as she closed the door behind her, she broke down crying. She didn't care if the man heard her. She couldn't believe that Kevin was gone. It was so much he didn't know. He didn't know that she came back. She had nothing to even remember him by. What would she tell her daughter when she asked about her daddy? As she finished using the bathroom and washing her face, the man banged on the door.

"Alight I'm coming." She wanted to punch the man in his mouth.

She walked out the bathroom passed him. He followed her into the living room. She stopped dead in her tracks and turned, "You don't have to follow me. I'm leaving asshole." When she stepped down the first step, she felt a sharp pain run through her stomach. She continued to walk. She doubted that if she called a cab it would arrive in time. She felt like the inside of her vagina was on fire. She sat on the steps, but that made it worst. She dialed 911 and told them operator she needed an ambulance. She managed to give the address before the pain became too bad. She couldn't stop moaning and gritting her teeth.

CHAPTER 17

When the paramedics arrived, Joy was at the bottom of the step clutching the rail. On the way to the hospital, Joy felt a strong sensation and then wetness run down her legs. The pain got worst and she couldn't take it, she screamed. After the paramedic noticed that Joy's water broke, he removed her pants. When he looked to see how much she was dilated, he yelled to the driver, "You have to go faster, I can see the head."

Joy freaked out. "What am I going to do? It's too early," she shouted. The paramedic tried to calm her down. He told her to hold her breath and push. She leaned back screaming, refusing to push. Joy paused her breath though. That worked for a few seconds. It was like her body worked against her, she pushed. She pushed again and the baby came right out. Joy felt such a relief until she realized that she didn't hear the baby crying like in the movies.

She opened her eyes to see what was going on. She watched as the paramedic, cleared the baby's airways. He performed the CPR as tears ran down Joy's face. "I can't lose you too," she whispered. She said it over like five times in a row, like a prayer. Seconds passed and finally she heard her baby's yell of life.

They arrived at the hospital. The baby was rushed to intensive care and Joy rushed to Labor and Delivery. After making sure that everything came out, she was taken to her room. The baby was so small that Joy didn't need any stitches.

"When can I see my baby?" Joy asked the nurse.

"I have to call down there. The doctor may want to come talk to you first but I'll let you know. The bracelet on your arm matches your daughter. You have to keep on until the baby leaves. That is the only way you can visit her in intensive care. As soon as I find out I'll let you know."

The nurse left and Joy laid back against the bed and closed her eyes. She couldn't believe everything happened so fast. She swung her legs over the side of the bed and stood up. Her legs were shaking. She held on the end of the bed to get her balance. She wrapped another gown over her, to cover the back and headed towards the nurses station.

She didn't see her nurse, but there were two nurses sitting there talking.

"Can I help?" one nurse asked.

"Can you tell me where the intensive care for babies is?"

"It's the floor below us. The elevators are straight and to the right."

Joy walked in the direction the nurse told her. When she reached the floor, she became nervous and her heart sped up. When she walked to the hallway outside the intensive care, there were other people standing there. She saw that they all had on yellow gowns. She went to the cabinet and took out a gown and put it on. She stood there, unsure about what to do next. The door opened and some people walked out and the people in the hall went in next, Joy followed them. They checked her wristband and asked her last name. She had to wash her hands and arms up to the elbow. The nurse then led her to "Baby girl Williams."

Joy looked at the baby's face and broke down. She was so tiny. The paper on the crib read 1lbs 7oz. The nurse asked the baby's name but Joy ignored her. Joy's bottom lip trembled, as the tears fell. She couldn't tell which daddy the baby looked like. She knew that the baby was beautiful.

The tears made everything blurry. She backed up, slowly. She went to the door and went out. Once she got back to her room, she found her clothes and put them on. She checked in her bag to make sure her money was there, it was. She stuck her head out the door. The nurses' station was empty, except for one person. Keeping her head down, she walked to the other side of the hospital to get to the front door.

When she got to the corner, there were people everywhere. Joy knew she looked crazy, her hair was all over her head. She tried to smooth it down with her hand. She just wanted to go to a hotel. She didn't want to go back to the apartment because she didn't want to explain what happened if she saw Simone.

The bus came headed towards Frankford Terminal. Joy remembered the time she was there, after Josh tried to kidnap her. He was her first love. Even though he constantly mistreated her, Joy still loved him with all her heart. The day she accidently shot him, the love she had for him seem to die with him. She paid and went straight to the back to sit by the window.

At the terminal, she got on the 14 towards Neshaminy Mall. She thought that she would find a place to stay on Roosevelt Blvd. She went straight to the back and leaned her head against the window. In seconds she dozed off. She opened her eyes just in time to see that she was almost at the last stop. She signaled to get off. She only had to walk a little ways up the street where she found a motel.

"Can I help you?" the man behind the window asked.

"Yea, I need a room."

"$5 an hour or $50 for the night."

Joy gave him enough for the week. He gave her the key and a remote. She walked passed the vendor machines. They were almost empty. She was glad that there were stores in the area.

The smell of dust hit Joy as she stepped through the door of her room. She plunged down on the bed. She kept seeing the baby's tiny face. She knew that she wouldn't be a good mother. She wished that her mother would have did the same. The baby would be better without her. Her heart ached and she needed something to take her mind off everything.

CHAPTER 18

It was only five-thirty. There was so much stuff that Joy needed, she decided to hop back on the bus to got to Wal-Mart. She didn't care that none of the stuff was name brand. She grabbed jeans, shorts, tee shirts and underwear. She got all the toiletries she would need. She even grabbed snacks and stuff to eat and drink, since the room had a mini fridge and microwave.

By the time she made it back to the room with the bags, she felt beyond exhausted. She plunked on the bed on top of the covers and went to sleep. She slept the whole night and most of the morning. Her head pounded from too much sleep. She sat up. The first thing she wanted to do was brush her teeth and take a shower. She searched through bags and gathered everything she needed.

Joy didn't know her next move but she figured that she would stay there until something came to her. Two weeks passed and still nothing came to her. She cried everyday. The only enjoyment she was that the bleeding stopped. During the time, Joy only left the room to go pay for another week.

She remembered she saw a beer place down the street. They said that they sold hoagies and cheese steaks; Joy went to check it out. When she walked in, all eyes were on her. She went to the counter and ordered a cheese fries and a burger. While she waited, she looked around at the different beers. She saw a case that said Twisted Tea on it. It was a 24 pack with different favorites. Joy decided to get that. She struggled with it up to the counter. After she paid for everything, she turned to leave. At the door she bumped into a man.

He was about 6'3". Joy had to look up to see his face. He had smooth dark skin like a special dark Hershey bar. His eyes were unlike she'd seen before. They were perfectly round and a deep brown. His lips looked smooth and kissable. He was kind of husky but in a muscular way. He had long dreads that hung passed his shoulders. She didn't even process his looks. She tried to continue pass him but he stopped her.

"Wait honey. You need help with that?"

Joy wanted to say no but shook her head yes.

"Where you taking this, to a party?"

"No I'm staying right there." Joy said pointing in the direction of the motel.

"What? You got me carrying your shit so you can hook up with ya nigga."

"Hold up...."

"It's cool, I was just playing. You don't even need to get upset."

"Oh."

When they got to the entrance, Joy reached for the drinks.

"I can carry them for you."

"Thank you, but I'm good here."

"I wont try to come in your room."

"Aight." Joy gave in, unsure.

He sat the case at the door for her. "Aight enjoy." He said, and started to walk away.

Suddenly something about him interested her. "Wait." she called to him. He stopped but didn't say anything.

"You didn't even tell me your name."

"Wayne. Yours?"

"Joy."

"Aight Joy, I'll see you around." He said and continued walking down the hall.

Joy went inside her room. She pulled the case up onto the dresser and opened it. She put some in the refrigerator to get cold. She turned on the TV and sat down to eat her food. She hadn't watched too much TV. She didn't want to see no babies or kids. Just the thought of seeing one made the sadness that now consumed her heart worst.

Joy had to turn the TV off and she couldn't finish her meal. She was bored and lonely. She thought about Kevin and the baby all the time. She refused to give the baby a name. She just wanted to forget. She wished that she would had told Kevin about the money. Maybe he wouldn't have gone to work that day.

She replayed the message he left over and over. She couldn't believe that she would hear his voice again. She didn't know if the baby was his or not. She even thought about going back to see her but couldn't bring her self to follow through. She only had to close her eyes to see her face.

CHAPTER 19

Joy could no longer stand to be in the room at the motel. She didn't even have any more clean clothes. She was wearing her last clean pair of under wear. She had to buy a trash bag from the lady vacuum the hallway, to put all her stuff in. She sat on the bed and finished off the cooler she was drinking. She couldn't remember how many she'd drunk. She wished that she had something stronger.

For days now, she'd been drinking case after case of coolers. She didn't know how many trips she made to the beer place. Since her initial visit, she didn't see Wayne. She wasn't really attracted to him but, he seemed to be the only dude she met in a while that didn't try to get at her.

She checked one last time to make sure that she got everything before she left. She had no place else to go but back to her apartment until she figured out what else to do. She still had the money. She knew that if she saw Simone, she would notice that Joy wasn't pregnant anymore. She would just tell her that she lost the baby and leave it at that. She would act like she was too upset to explain what happened.

As Joy walked to the bus stop, she heard someone beep at her. She turned and looked in that direction but then kept walking. She heard someone yelling, "Aye."

She sucked her teeth. *This dude won't give up*. Then she felt him tap her on the shoulder. "Hold up," she turned around and was surprised to see it was Wayne.

He looked different. He had a low cut. His dreads were gone.

"I didn't even know that was you. What happened?" she asked, pointing at his head.

"I needed a change," he said simply, like it was no big deal to him.

Joy studied his features. She could tell that he was at least in his mid thirties.

"I'm surprised to see you still here. I was driving by here on the way to pick my daughter up from the movies, when I spotted you."

"Oh." Joy said.

She looked in time to see the bus coming, but she wasn't even close to the stop. She was mad that he made her miss the bus but didn't show it. When she turned around, he was staring at her. She became self-conscience. Her clothes were wrinkled. Her hair pulled back into a ponytail.

"Yo, you need a ride somewhere?" he asked, breaking the silence.

"Yeah," Joy wasn't trying to wait for another bus.

They hopped in his car. He had a two door Nissan Sentra. Outside his car showed it's age but on the inside everything appeared new. He had leather seats and plush carpet on the floors. The dashboard was wood and he had a CD player with a radio that named each song and artist that came on.

"Which way you headed?"

"Cottman and Bustleton."

"Ok."

He drove off in that direction. They were headed in the opposite direction of the mall. He said that he was picking up his daughter. Joy wondered if he was lying or was he making his own daughter wait, just to get at her. She dismissed it and decided she didn't care one way or the other.

He turned the music up so loud that Joy felt the bass in her ears. He was playing some old school rap; singing along word from word. Joy was glad that he was doing like 80 the whole way because she couldn't wait to get out the car.

Just when Joy thought she couldn't take the noise any more, he turned it down.

"So where you headed?"

"Cottman and Bustleton."

"Yea I know. But like to your man's house or something?"

"No." Joy kept it short. She didn't understand why he just didn't ask if she had a man or not. Instead of trying to get her to tell him.

"You stay out there?"

"Yeah."

"You kind of quiet."

They had reached Joy's destination.

"Wait." he said when Joy went to open the door.

"Is there something wrong with me?" He asked.

Joy wanted to say yeah but shook her head no.

"I know you know I'm trying to get at you, but you acting like you're not interested. What you got a man?"

"No. I'm just going through some things."

"You girls kill me with that. Why can't yall be real?"

Joy didn't answer him. She was lost in thought. She was thinking about just hopping on Greyhound and starting over some place else.

"Yo, you heard me?"

"No. What you say?" Joy said, her voice deflated.

"Can I get your number? Maybe if we talk, you'll see I'm really a good dude."

Joy gave him her number only because she didn't know anyone else. She reasoned that he might become useful in the near future.

"I can take you to your house."

"I'm good here."

She got out of the car and crossed the street. She walked into the Sears and loaded a cart with everything she could think that she needed for her apartment. She even brought a blowup mattress to use until she got a bed. She spent over $1700. With no way to get it home, she pushed the cart all the way home.

It took several trips to take everything in her apartment. She took her time and put everything up. She then realized that she left her bag in Wayne's car. She might have talked him up, she thought, looking at the screen on her phone. The number was blocked.

"Hello." Joy answered.

"Yo, What you doing?"

"Nothing."
"You want to get something to eat?"
"Umm, sure why not."
"I'll be there in a hour."
Joy hung up and jumped in the shower.

Joy was dressed and ready in 30 minutes. She didn't ask where they were going because any place was better than being cooped up in the house. When he called and said he was outside, Joy went out and got in the car. She never questioned the fact that she didn't give him the direction to her apartment building.

CHAPTER 20

They rode in silence, no music, no talking, nothing. Joy started to ask where they were going, when Wayne asked, "Do you want to get out this heat?"

Joy thought that was a weird question to ask but answered yes. Three blocks later, he pulled over and parked the car. He jumped out of the car. Joy looked around for a few seconds before she got out. Wayne was already at the front door to a house. He took out some keys and opened the door. Joy followed him in. She didn't understand why they were here but she didn't ask any questions.

She sat on the sofa. The first thing she noticed was how neat everything was. The hardwood floors shined, not one drop of dirt or dust. The mirrors and the glass tabletops were the same. It was a row home, so everything was on the same floor. Joy watched Wayne in the kitchen, pouring them something to drink.

He came back with some red kool aid. "We are still going to eat because I'm starving." she said and took a sip.

"Yea. I thought we watch a movie and order out. We could get a few different things like pizza and Chinese, or whatever.

"You can just take me back."

"You tripping. Take you back. How you sound?"

"I'm not playing."

"Look. Relax. Go in the room and pick out a movie."

Joy took out her phone to call a cab. She didn't know what she was thinking by even coming the house with him in the first place.

Wayne got up and went into the bedroom. He walked back out, with a stack of movies. He handed them to Joy. She relaxed when she realized that he wasn't trying to lure her into his bedroom. She looked at them. He had all the new movies. She picked out the Beyonce movie *Obsessed*.

"I want to watch this one," she said, handing him the movie.

"Ok. Did you decide what you want to eat?"

"No. You pick."

He ordered an extra large cheese pizza, Buffalo wings, onion rings and two strawberry milkshakes. Joy was so engrossed in the movie, she didn't look away when Wayne handed her the food and drink.

When the movie was over, Wayne asked, "Do you want to watch another movie?"

"Umm." Joy suddenly had trouble talking. She couldn't think clearly. "I. I. You." She tried to stand up. Her knees buckled and she fell. She stayed still, fighting to keep her eyes open. Seconds later, blackness surrounded her.

The next time Joy opened her eyes she was on her air mattress, in her apartment. She tried to sit up but fell back from the sharp pains shooting through her head. She was fully dress, she even had on her sneakers. She looked around, realizing she was in her apartment. The bag of clothes she had left in Wayne's car was sitting in the corner. She didn't want to move but she had to pee quickly. She rolled onto the floor and crawled her way into the bathroom. Her entire body ached. She leaned against the bathroom door and kicked off her sneakers. Her pants were unbuckled but she had trouble getting them off.

She had some discomfort in her vagina. She thought it was normal to have pain from time to time because she just had a baby not too long ago. It burned when she peed.

She soaked for forty-five minutes in the tub and that helped a little. As she was drying off, she looked in the mirror and noticed that her eyes were blood shot. She had deep bags under her eyes. She didn't want to do nothing but climb back in the bed. So she did and slept the rest of the day. When she woke up, she laid there, staring in the dark for another hour and a half, thinking about what could have happened before she got up. She wanted to get something to eat but her stomach felt funny and nauseous.

She searched for her cell phone. She had twelve missed calls, all from a private number. She didn't have any menus so she couldn't order anything, she would have to go out or see if one of her neighbors had anything. The phone vibrated in her hands. She was sitting on the edge of the air mattress, looking down. It was a private number. She didn't feel like talking to anyone, she pressed ignore. Five seconds later there was a knock on the door.

She walked tiptoed to the door and looked through the peephole. Wayne stood outside the door. He had his phone in his hand. She waited, hoping he would go away.

But he continued to knock. Finally she opened the door enough to stick her head out.

"Joy Was sup?"

"Now is not a good time."

"Yeah? You got company?" he asked trying to look behind her in the door.

"No and I don't really want none either."

"Joy why you acting like that. I came all the way over here to check on you and you being nasty."

"Check on me why?"

"I had a bad case of food poisoning from the food we ate. Since I know we ate the same thing, I figure you was sick too."

"I was with you?"

"Yeah I dropped you off here last night. Don't you remember?"

"Damn. I was pretty fucked up I guess."

"You going to let me in? I got something that will make you feel better." He said, holding up two glass jars of haze.

Joy thought about it for a second. She did crave the relaxed feeling she knew that she would get from smoking. Without saying a word, she opened the door wide enough for Wayne to enter.

"Yo, you need some furniture in this bitch. My man got a living room set for sale. Sofa, tables and all that, I can hook you up," he said looking around the living room.

"I'll let you know."

"You got something to eat."

"I don't have anything in my refrigerator. I was going to order out but I guessing that wouldn't be a good idea."

"We can run to the market. I can cook for you."

"Yea okay." You can cook?"

"What. I'm a gourmet chef."

Joy laughed. "Alright let me get dressed."

"Naw, you can go like that."

She looked down at her pajama bottoms and shrugged. She stuck her feet into her flip-flops and followed Wayne out the door.

CHAPTER 21

When they returned, Wayne made his famous dish, tacos. Joy couldn't stop laughing, as she watched him make them. "Some gourmet chef," she joked, enjoying her time with him.

"Make jokes all you want. You have never had tacos like these in your young life. I even got dessert." He pulled a Duncan Hines box from the bag.

Joy saw that it was double fudge chocolate and got excited. It had been a while since she had cake.

"That looks like it's going to be good," she said as she walked to the bathroom. When she came back, Wayne had mixed the cake and put it in the oven. Dinner was done and Wayne rolled up. In no time, he had four blunts lined on the table.

Joy had laid down pillows and blankets on the floor. She placed all the food in the middle, like a picnic. Wayne lit up one of the blunts, took a few hits and passed to Joy. She had no trouble as she inhaled and held the smoke. She let it out easy. She did this a few times before she passed it back, but Wayne waved her away as he lit another one.

With no astray, Joy jumped up and got a bowl from the kitchen. She put the L down and stuffed a taco full of meat, lettuce, tomatoes, and cheese. She poured sour cream and taco sauce on the top. On her first bite, she swore she never tasted anything so good in her life. She took turns eating and smoking. After 20 minutes, Joy's mouth was dry. They forgot to get something to drink; she filled two cups of water from the faucet and gave one to Wayne.

After three slices of cake, she was so full all she could do was lay back on the blanket and stare at the ceiling. By then the weed was gone and Wayne wanted to go to the store and get some liquor. He asked Joy to ride with him but she couldn't move. So, he went by his self.

Hours passed and Wayne hadn't come back. Joy still was in the same spot. Finally, Joy rolled on her side and went to sleep.

A sharp, burning pain shot through Joy's stomach waking her up out of a deep sleep. She jumped up and ran to the bathroom, barely making in it time as watery liquid shot out of her. Just when she thought she was done and was walking out the bathroom, she had to run right back in. She plopped on the toilet, trying to figure out what could be wrong. First the food poisoning and now she had diarrhea.

Her trips became less frequent. After an hour passed she continued to go off and on all day. Once she was sure that she was done, she hopped in the shower. She heard someone knocking on the door when she got out. She hurried to get dressed. The person knocked louder. “Hold on,” she yelled. She caught herself smiling at the thought of Wayne at the door and relaxed her face.

She went to the door and looked through the peephole. “Shit.” She stared at Simone for a moment and then opened the door.

“Girl, I didn’t think you was ever going to open the door,” Simone said. Walking through the door she took a double look at Joy and then looked away. Joy grew more nervous as Simone continued, “Where you been? I came down here a couple times.” She continued not waiting for answers. “ I wanted to see if you needed anything.”

“I’m okay.”

“Well I don’t want to hold you up. You know where I’m at if you need something.” She turned, her hand on the knob. “Joy what happened to the baby?” she asked.

Joy thought she wasn’t going to ask. She wasn’t mad at her. She was there the day Joy first found out she was pregnant and when Joy had no one else there to support her. She wanted to tell her the truth. She stood there. The words froze in her throat. Tears fell down her face. She tried not to think about what she did.

"I lost the baby. She came too early." Joy looked away. She couldn't look Simone in the eyes. Simone came over and pulled Joy to her. Simone used the back of her hand to wipe away Joy's tears. A few minutes passed, Joy tried to back up but Simone held onto her.

Their faces were so close, that Joy could feel her breath on her face. Simone leaned in and kissed Joy's lips. Joy kissed her back. She felt Simone push her tongue in her mouth. Surprisingly, Joy thought of Wayne and stepped back.

They started at each other. Neither got a chance to say anything because there was a knock the door. Since Simone was closest to the door, she opened it. Ronnie stood there.

"What you doing down here?"

"I was just coming down here to check on Joy."

"Why you wait until I fell asleep?"

"Look, go down the hall and we can talk about it."

Joy, still stun, stood there after they left.

CHAPTER 22

A few days went by and Joy spent half the time thinking about Wayne and half the time thinking about Simone. She thought about the kiss she had with Simone. She didn't know if she liked it on it's own or was it because during it she started thinking about Wayne. She didn't kiss him yet. She tried not to think about the situation because she wanted to try to be friends with him. She didn't think that she was ready for more, so soon after Kevin. She was still confused about the kiss. If she did like it, did that make her gay? She wondered what would have happened if Ronnie never came to the door.

She was bored sitting in the house so she decided to do some shopping. She was walking up to Cottman to get the bus, when she walked passed three cars that were for sale. The one in the middle stood out to her. It was a red Grand Am. The paint job looked new and Joy pictured herself riding around in it. She wasn't sure that she should call the number. She didn't have a license and she knew nothing about buying a car.

She weighed her options. She did need a car. She dialed the number and waited for someone to answer.

"Hello." a nasally voice answered.

"Yeah, um I'm calling about the red Grand Am you have for sale."

"Okay. Its $1800 and you have to pay for tags and registration up front."

"Never mind," Joy said and hung up.

She continued walking down the street. Her cell phone rang. It was the same man from before.

"Hello." She answered.

"Well what's the problem? We could probably work something out."

"I don't know. I don't have a license."

"Then why you trying to buy a car?" he asked before he hung up on her.

Joy hopped on the bus and went to Raymoor and Flanigan. She picked out a red leather sofa and two red leather recliners with two lamps. She got a glass coffee table and two glass end tables to match. She purchased an entertainment center for the new 52" TV. She also got a queen-size bed and a dresser and two nightstands to go in her room. After paying nine thousand, they set up and delivery date for two days later. Joy was on her way.

Her next stop was the Penn Dot. She had no interest in getting her license but she did need some identification other than her school. She waited in line, took her picture for a state ID, waited some more and then walked out with her new ID.

From there she went straight to the bank. She decided to open up an safety deposit box. She couldn't walk around with all the money on her. She was slipping the other day when she woke up in her apartment, unable to remember what was going on. She could lose everything by being careless, and then where would she be?

She filled out the paper work. She had to open a bank account first. She put in enough money to pay the safety deposit box up to six months. Placing the money in the box, she exited with twenty thousand.

By the time she made it back to her apartment, it was well into the evening. She loaded the clothes in the washer and dryer because she had yet to go food shopping. She didn't know what she would eat. She was starving after not eating anything all day. She wondered about Wayne. She thought about him all day and constantly looked at her phone hoping he would call. He didn't give her a number to reach him. She would go by his house but she couldn't remember where it was.

He hadn't called in days. She hated that she didn't have any way to get in contact with him. It was like he had all the power and she lost the power she had. They weren't in a relationship, but Joy enjoyed the last time she spent with him. She wished that she had grabbed something to eat while she was out because she didn't feel like going back out. She drank two glasses of water and tried to forget about it. For some reason Joy felt dirty. She walked to her bedroom, jumped in the shower and washed the sweat and dirt of the day off. She even washed her hair. She changed the sheets on her air mattress. She felt comfortable as she dozed off to sleep.

The next morning when Joy woke up, she felt well rested. She looked at the phone for any missed calls from Wayne. There were none. The good feeling she had left. A million thoughts ran through her mind. She couldn't understand why Wayne hadn't called in four days. She needed something to get her mind on something else. She thought about Kevin and the baby. She felt guilty that she was already moving on with her life. She didn't know what else to do. She hated to be alone.

CHAPTER 23

Joy was again tired of sitting around the house. Her furniture wasn't coming until the next day and she needed to get out. She locked the door and walked to the elevator. She saw Simone standing there. She had funny feeling in her stomach from nervousness. She hadn't seen her since the kiss they shared.

Simone had her back to Joy but turned around when she heard Joy walk up. Simone tried to smile but Joy was speechless. The whole right side of Simone's face was swollen and both of her eyes were black. Joy could tell that Simone tried to hide it under the layers of makeup caked on her face but it only covered it a little bit.

"What happened to your face?" Joy screamed pulling back the hair that Simone tried to cover it.

"Oh my God," she said, the bruises looked worst up close. "That bitch Ronnie did this, didn't she?"

Simone shook her head yes; tears falling down her cheeks. Simone, the strong go-getter seemed defeated.

"I can't believe that she beat you," Joy said, sucking her teeth. They were standing in front of the building. Simone looked up and down the street, looking for Ronnie.

"She was so mad. I never seen her so mad." Simone spoke for the first time since Joy met her in the hall.

"What happened?"

Simone hesitated but answered, "She caught me fucking the brother Jamek."

Joy's mouth opened but nothing came out. Many thoughts ran through her head at once, she didn't know what to say. She didn't even know Simone was in to dudes. Joy wondered why she kissed her and then fucks Jamek. Joy was quiet for to long and Simone started crying.

"I hope I'm not crossing a line but why would you even do some shit like that?"

"I don't know. I was high on X and it just happened. Ronnie walked in on us in the living room. She came at him with a knife and he ran out the door butt-naked. I was still high when she beat my ass."

"Damn that's some crazy shit." Joy said, ready to go on about her business. She was ready to ride with Simone and kick Ronnie's ass but she couldn't fault Ronnie. This explained why Ronnie was so crazy jealous. No telling how many men or women Simone cheated on Ronnie with. Joy made a mental note to keep her distance from Simone. She wasn't trying to get caught up in her drama.

"I hope you feel better. I have to go. I'll see you later."

"Okay. Bye."

Joy walked off in the direction of the bus stop. Simone was still standing in front of the building. She had no real agenda. She went to look in the stores at Roosevelt Mall. She window-shopped but did purchase a few outfits and shoes from Joyce Leslie's. She got some food to take out from the Chinese Buffet and headed back home.

Wayne was getting out of his car as she walked up to the building. He smiled at her as they met at the steps. Joy kept her face straight and serious. She didn't want him to know that she was happy to see him. She didn't even understand the feeling of happiness she got every time she was around him.

He carried her bags for her. They entered the apartment. Joy dropped her bags in the bedroom and walked back out to the living room, where Wayne was standing. She studied his features for a moment. She didn't know anything about him. What kind of job he had? How many kids he had, nothing? And he didn't know anything about her either.

They sat on the floor and shared the food that Joy got earlier. They laughed and joked.

"Don't you want to go out?"

"Not really." Joy said enjoying the time they were spending together.

"Come on. I have the perfect place for us to go."

"Alright, lets go."

They were on their way down highway 95. Joy looked out the window. It was getting dark out and Joy couldn't see much. "Where we going?" she asked.

"AC." he answered.

"Really?" Joy was so excited. She couldn't wait to get there and couldn't help but thank about the time she went with Shawn. They didn't go into any of the casinos, just the mall down there.

Wayne pulled into the Trump Plaza's parking, paid the four dollars and found a spot to park. When Joy walked into the casino in awe. The lights were so bight. The carpet had a checkered pattern. The noises from the machines excited her even more. She couldn't wait to play. There were so many people. Some smoking, some with drinks in their hands. Women in skimpy outfits walked around shouting "coffee, tea, beverages." Wayne warned her to be careful. He knew that she wasn't twenty-one yet and she wasn't supposed to be in the casino.

Joy walked around looking at the machines. She couldn't decide what to play. She was a little nervous about security but none of them said a word to her. She began to relax. She settled on a machine called Wheel of Fortune. It was a quarter to play. The max bet was three quarters. At first Joy tried to put a dollar in the machine but it wouldn't go. When she realized that you could only put dominations of fives, tens, twenties, fifties or hundreds, she was embarrassed that she didn't know or read the sign first. She looked around to see if anyone was watching and laughed at her self.

Wayne went off to play blackjack. As soon as Joy put in her twenty and hit the Max button, the machine shouted "Wheel Of Fortune." She hit the button that was lit and looked up to watch where the spinner stopped. It stopped on 1000. She had no idea how much that was until she added up. "What's 1000 quarters?" she said out loud as she thought about it.

"$250!" She screamed.

She continued to play and gambled away the whole $250. She wanted to try something else, hit the cash out button and watched a piece of paper come out. She had $75 left. She saw Wayne walking towards her.

"Boo, I need to borrow some money. I lost a little more than I wanted but I can make it back if you let me get that." he yelled over the noise.

"He called me boo." Joy thought, happy. She handed him the voucher she just received. He looked down at it. "This is not enough."

Joy dug in her bag and pulled out $200 dollars. Before she could put her hand out to give it to him, he took out her hand, kissed her cheek and walked away. He didn't give her back the voucher.

She continued to walk around, playing every machine that seemed fun. She didn't win anything else. She would win a little but play it right back and then move on to the next machine.

Joy checked her phone for the time and saw that it was 1:47 in the morning. She walked around, trying to spot Wayne. She didn't see him at none of the tables. She made a stop at the bathroom, got a coke, tipped the lady and continued to walk around. There was no sign of Wayne. The place was still packed with people. She wasn't sure if she kept missing him, so she went back to the place where he left her before; figuring that he was probably would go there to look for her.

All the machines were taken. She had nothing to do as she stood there and waited. It was 3:36 am. She had the idea to go to where he parked and meet him there. As she walked, she couldn't help but wonder why he just didn't call her and they meet up.

She had her answer by the time she made back to the spot he parked. His car was no longer there. Joy stood in the empty space, sure that was where he had parked. Tears welled up in her eyes. "Why did he leave me?"

she wondered. She didn't know what to do. She went back inside the casino. She saw a sign for the bus, so she went in that direction.

She reached the counter. She asked how to get a bus to Philadelphia. The lady told her where the bus depot was near Bally's casino to buy a ticket. Joy walked, crying the whole way. Her feelings were hurt. Her throat hurt, she cried hard.

She purchased her ticket. When the bus arrived, she made sure to be the first one on. She went all the way to the back to where there were three seats. She put her legs across them, leaned her back against the window, turned her face towards the seat and cried the whole way to Philly.

CHAPTER 24

Joy was last to get off the bus at Board and Olney. The sun was coming up. She was glad that she knew where she was, having been there before. People were already at the bus stops trying to get to work.

She hopped on the bus when it came. Her stop came and she got off and hopped on another to take her closer to her house. The whole time, she willed her self not to think about Wayne. By then, she had stopped crying about it. She got off the elevator in her building. She walked pass Simone's door. Clothes were piled outside her door. Joy guessed Ronnie's because it looked like a bunch of man's jeans and T-shirts.

Once inside, she went straight to her room, dropped her bag on the floor and decided to lay down. She didn't bother to remove her clothes. Exhausted, she fell asleep right away.

Two weeks passed, still no Wayne. He didn't call or come by. Her furniture arrived the same day that she arrived back home the next day after Wayne ditched her. She spent days watching TV and ordering pizza.

She was depressed over Wayne. She didn't understand why. They hadn't had sex yet. She needed someone to talk to but had no one. Simone was out of the question. The phone rang and she jumped up and ran to her bedroom where it was charging. She looked at the screen and saw a block number. She reminded herself that she was mad answered with attitude. "Yeah."

"Hey sexy," he said as if nothing happened.

"Who is this?"

"Stop playing, you know who this is."

"What you want?"

"Damn it's like that. Where's the love?"

"It's real funny that you say that cause I want to know where the love was when ya ass left me in Atlantic City," Joy said and hung up. She was furious. She thought he would apologize and have a good reason for leaving her stranded but he acted as if the shit didn't happen.

Half and hour later, Wayne was at the door. He knocked. Joy looked out the peephole and stood at the door.

"Joy listen, you didn't give me a chance to explain. I left you that night because my grandma went to the hospital. She had the swine flu. She almost died."

Joy didn't know whether to believe him or not. He could have made it up because he knew she was mad. "He did come all the way over here just to tell me, maybe he do feel something for me," she reasoned to herself.

"Is she okay?" she asked through the door.

"Yea, she just came home today. As soon as I got her straight I called you."

Joy opened the door and let him in. He grinned and leaned in to kiss her but she backed away. "I'm still mad. You could have at least called me or found me."

"I know Joy. But I panicked. I did try to find you, but after a half an hour I had to leave. I made it back to Philly in like 45 minutes. That's how fast I was going."

"I guess I can't fault you for that. I'm glad I had a way home and that your grandma is better."

They were still standing at the door. Wayne was talking about the furniture. She watched his lips and she could only think of one thing. She stood on her tipsy toes and kissed him. He kissed her back, griping her butt with both hands. They kissed for a long time. By the time they stopped, the area around Joy's lips was red.

She stepped out of pants and pulled him by the hand, leading him into the bedroom.

"Damn." he said, looking around at Joy's bedroom. "You hooked your living room and bedroom up."

Joy didn't answer. She pushed him back on the bed and finished removing her clothes. Wayne rushed to unbuckle his belt. He took off all his clothes, except his wife beater. He reached out and tugged at one of Joy's nipples. Joy looked down at his hard dick. It was about six inches, but it was thick as hell.

The tip was so fat that it filled Joy's mouth. Wayne moaned like he was about to cum. He stopped Joy and pulled her next to him. He started kissing her neck. Joy couldn't wait. She reached down and started jerking his dick, getting it ready. She moved until he back to give him access. She briefly thought about stopping and making him put on a condom but she didn't.

He placed his dick at the outside of her opening. He placed both Joy's feet on his chest. He slid into her wetness and they both moaned from the impact of pleasure. Joy closed her eyes tight. She bit down on her lip, trying not to scream too loud. Wayne was sweating all over but she didn't care because he was hitting every spot he was supposed to.

He pulled out and motioned for Joy to roll over. He pulled her back on her knees in the position he wanted and slid back in. Joy's pussy muscles were working over time. Her spot started to tingle and she yelled out, "Shit, I'm bout to cum."

Her body tightened up and she started shaking as the organism ran through her body. Wayne kept right on stroking her harder and harder. Another strong sensation shot through her body. Joy fell on her stomach because she couldn't take anymore. Wayne stroked his dick, allowing Joy to catch her breath.

He rolled her on her side, moved behind her and entered again. Joy looked over her shoulder and had to hold back her laugh at the facial expression on Wayne's face. He had an intense look of concentration. Joy didn't like the position because her back hurt. Just when she was about to tell him, he pulled out and came on her hip.

He collapsed beside her. Joy reached on the nightstand and grabbed some tissue. She handed it to Wayne and then got some and wiped herself off.

"Yo, can you get me something to drink?"

Joy ran to the kitchen and filled a cup with water. When she gave it to Wayne he had a problem. He didn't want water but that was all she had. She tried to tell him but he was already mad. He turned his back on her and went to sleep. Joy laid staring at his back for an hour, unable to sleep. She didn't understand why he would get so mad over something like that. It wasn't like she purposely didn't give him something different to drink. She had yet to go food shopping.

Joy dozed off after another half hour of trying to make sense of Wayne's bizarre behavior.

CHAPTER 25

When Joy woke up the next morning, Wayne was gone. He didn't leave a note or nothing. Disappointed, she got out the bed to take a shower. A deep sadness filled her heart. Today was her nineteenth birthday and she wanted to spend it with Wayne. She didn't have a number where she could reach him.

She sucked her teeth as she thought about how Wayne could just leave without saying anything to her. After she finished drying off, she changed her sheets. She was about to lay down again, when her phone rang. She looked down at the display screen and saw the same number that someone been calling her from for the last three days. Opening her phone, she answered just as the call was about to go to voicemail.

"Hello." she answered. No one said anything.

"Hello." she repeated.

She waited, listening to see if she could make out any background noises. She closed her phone and laid back on her pillow. For the last three days, whoever was calling her would call at the same time. They wouldn't say anything they would just listen.

Rolling over on her side, preparing to go back to sleep, her phone rang again. She opened her phone and answered, "Hello."

"Was sup?" she heard Wayne asked."

"Nothing. Why you leave like that?"

"Like what?"

"You didn't even wake me up to say bye. You just rolled out."

"Yeah I know."

"You know? That's all you got to say?"

"I'm will call you right back."

"Wait a minute."

"What?"

"Today's my birthday and I want to do something with you."

"Aight. We can do something later. I'll call you." He hung up, not allowing Joy to fit in another word.

Joy closed her phone with a huge smile on her face. She found something to wear and laid it out on her bed. She put on a clean pair of pajamas, opting to wait to later to Wayne called back to get dressed. She went out into the living room to watch TV, to pass the time. She watched judge shows the rest of the day. She had the phone right by her on the armrest. Wayne never called. It was starting to get dark outside.

She felt so stupid for allowing him to treat her this. He lied to her. "He probably had a wife or something. What other reason would there be for the way he acted and for him not to give her his number?" She was going to ask him for it to see what he says.

After turning everything off, she went into her bedroom. She pushed the clothes on the floor and got in. She couldn't fight the tears that were streaming down her face. She tried to hold in the noise but the sobbing noises escaped. She pressed her face into the pillow and screamed at the top of her lungs.

She cried the rest of the night. In the morning her eyes were stuck together and her head pounded from lack of sleep. The sadness in her heart weighed her down. *Why can't I ever be happy*? She wondered what excuse Wayne would use this time. She would have to stay in the dark because she made up her mind that she wasn't going to talk to him no more.

Despite everything that's happened since she met Wayne, she was starting to fall for him. By his actions, she knew that he couldn't feel the same. She knew that if she allowed herself to talk to him, he would give her some bullshit excuse that she would fall for.

While in the bathroom brushing her teeth, she heard someone at her door. She stood in the doorway and listened to Wayne talk to her through the door.

"Joy. Joy. I know you're in there and I'm not going nowhere till you talk to me."

She rinsed her mouth and walked to the door. She looked out the peephole and her only thought was how sexy he looked in his jeans, shorts and wife beater.

Joy went against the voice and her head telling her no and opened the door. The first thing she noticed was that he had huge bandage on his forehead.

"Oh my God, what happened to your head?"

"Man some niggas broke in my house and robbed me. One of them smacked me with the gun."

"Did you call the cops?"

"Naw I handled it already. I need you to come back and help me clean up."

"Ok." Joy ran into her room and put the clothes that were on the floor on. She back in the living room in three minutes.

Wayne had Joy drive to his house. It wasn't that far, so in no time they were there. Joy parked and they got out.

"How did they get in?" Joy asked, noticing that there was no damage to the front door.

"The front door but I got it fixed this morning."

"Ok," she said and followed Wayne through the front door.

Joy walked in, looked around and saw no mess or damage. She looked in the dining area there were dozen of balloons and a huge cake. A dozen roses sat next to it. Joy covered her face with her hand. She couldn't believe that he did this. It didn't matter that it was a day late.

She turned around towards him. "What, the robbery story was a lie?"

"Yeah. I was mad busy yesterday and I felt bad."

"This is wonderful. Thank you."

He walked to her and kissed her cheek but she turned her face into a wet and juicy kiss. He lifted her unto the table and pulled her underwear off, leaving her skirt on. He unzipped his jeans and entered her. He held both her legs as he pumped in and out of her. He picked her up off the table and carried her to the bedroom.

He laid Joy on the bed and took his pants off. He got in bed, rolling onto his back and told Joy get on top. Joy eased down on his dick and watched him bite his bottom lip. He pushed up into her as she rode him slow at first and then picking up speed when she was about to cum.

"Shiiitttt," she yelled out as she came.

A few more pumps from Wayne and he lifted Joy off him as he came. His chest heaved up and down as he caught his breath. Joy laid down beside him, stretching her the cramp she had in her leg.

"Can you get me some juice?"

Joy didn't feel like moving but she climbed over Wayne and went into the kitchen. She saw a cup in the dish drainer. She grabbed the cup and then went into the refrigerator and fetched a container filled with juice. She filled the cup to the top. She walked into the bedroom, trying not to spill it, only to find that Wayne was asleep.

Joy put the cup to her lips and drunk the juice without taking a breath. She was wide-awake. She wanted to find out more about him. Instead of asking him, she searched through his stuff.

Starting with his pants pockets, she pulled out his wallet. His license read Dwayne Curry. He was thirty-two. There was nothing else of interest in his wallet. No pictures of his kids or a wife. She placed it back in his pocket. She went to his closest and looked at the clothes that he had but there was only jeans and sneakers.

She pushed her clothes aside and looked for anything hidden in the back. She came up empty. She stepped back and looked at the shelf over the rack, then noticed a shoebox. She reached up, grabbed the shoebox and went to the living room to open it.

Lifting the lid, she held her breath, nervous about what she would find. A stack of cards, together in a rubber band was all that was in the box. She took them apart and looked at them. They were driving licenses: each of them had Wayne's face with different names and information.

Joy's eyes opened in shock. She continued to go through the cards. There was one for every state. She couldn't believe it. *Wayne might even be his real name.*

She wrapped the rubber band back around the cards, closed the shoebox and went to put it back. She almost dropped the box putting it back. She looked down and saw that it was a slit between the bedroom carpets that led into the closest. She looked behind her to make sure that Wayne was still sleep. She lifted up the carpet.

Under it was a piece in the floor that looked like it could be lifted up. She almost missed it. Joy went into the kitchen to get a butter knife. She came back, stuck it under and popped up the floor. Inside, there was an envelop with a disk in it. She pulled the disk out and saw her name written across it, the feeling of shock caused her to shake. She had to go to the bathroom because she felt like she was going to piss on herself.

She fixed everything the way she found. After hiding the disk in her bag, she got in the bed beside Wayne. She tried to tell her self to act normal until she could get home and see what was on the DVD. She moved over as far as she could away from him and listened to his breathing. She thought about waking him up and asking him to take her home.

After twenty minutes of trying to stay still, she eased out the bed and went into the living room. She got the DVD back out her bag and went to the TV. She grabbed the remote and turned the TV on, placing it on mute. She stuck the disk in and waited.

She saw Wayne's bedroom. The front of the bed was in view. Next, she saw Wayne carrying her in. He removed all his clothes and then removed all of Joy's. Joy's eyes grew wide with shock. She had her hand over her mouth to keep from making any noise. In the video, Joy's eyes were closed and her body was limp.

She remembered the day that she woke up and couldn't remember what happen. She now knew why. She watched as he had her sprawled out on the bed. He held her legs apart over her head and had sex with her. She watched until the end, where he pulled out and came in his hand. He left out the room and came back on the screen with a rag and cleaned Joy off.

Joy took it out and put it back in her bag. She turned off the TV. Something sick inside of Joy was turned on by what she just saw. Most people would freak out, but Joy wanted to know more about what Wayne was into.

CHAPTER 26

Joy nabbed her phone out her bag and went back into the bedroom. She put the phone on vibrate then went to Wayne's pants and got out his phone. She fumbled the phone as she looked at Wayne to make sure he was still sleep. She watched his chest move up and down for a few seconds. She dialed her number form his phone and looked down at her phone. His number still came up block. She thought that he was blocking his number when he called her but it was listed as blocked.

She was tried to see if the number to the phone was listed somewhere in the phone when someone called. The name Tee flashed on the screen. She fumbled, trying to silence the phone before it woke Wayne up and accidentally answered it. She put the phone up to her ear and listened. Joy thought that maybe it was a girlfriend or something by the way the person shouted in the phone.

"Daron, I been calling you. Why you not calling me back? I want that done tonight," the woman shouted. Joy didn't need to listen anymore. She recognized Tanya's voice and she knew that she walking about her. She hung up the phone and went into the kitchen. Joy paced back in forth and wondered what they had planned for her.

She heard Wayne call out from the bedroom. She jumped at the sound of his voice. She tried to fix her face and make sure she had a calm expression before she went back into the bedroom.

"Damn, I aint mean to fall asleep. You ready for me to take you home?" he asked as got up and walked to the bathroom. Joy used that opportunity to run in the kitchen, grab the biggest knife she saw and put it in her bag. She sat on the bed when he came back.

"You aight?" Wayne asked.

"Yeah. Why?"

"You got this funny look on your face."

"No. I'm good. Just a little tired."

"Ok. I'm sorry you didn't even get a chance to cut your cake but you can take it with you."

"Ok." Joy said.

"You sure you okay. You being kind of short."

"I'm good."

Joy followed behind Wayne out the bedroom and watched him pick the cake up, grab the balloons and they left out. He placed everything in the back seat of the car and they got in.

She waited for him to start driving. She reached over and started rubbing his dick through his jeans.

"Girl, what you doing?" Wayne asked getting excited.

"Nothing, keep driving." Joy undid his buckle and zipper, pulling out his rock hard dick. She stroked it with one hand as she reached in her bag for the knife. She wrapped her hand around the top of his dick and placed the knife at the bottom. When Wayne felt the coldness, he jumped. "What the fuck?" he looked down and nearly shit his self.

"Don't stop driving." Joy demanded when she noticed he slowed down.

"Joy what's happening?"

"What's happening is, if you don't tell me what the fuck is going on I will cut this little muthafucka off."

"Joy you tripping. Let my shit go."

"Daron, I'm not repeating myself."

"Shit. How did you...?"

"That don't matter. I know more than you think I do. Start talking," she tightened her grip.

"Aight look. Tanya's my cousin. She wanted me to come down here and fuck with you a little bit. It was her idea about the laxative and to leave you stranded down AC."

Tears fell out Joy's eyes. She was more angry than hurt. "What about this?" Joy said, holding up the DVD. Daron's eyes open in shock.

"How did you get that?"

"Call it luck. Now answer my question."

"Yeah."

"What are you supposed to do to me tonight?"

"I was supposed to plant a gun with a body on it in your apartment. Then make an anonymous call to the cops."

"Why was you so willing to do all this?" Joy said, starting to get choked up with emotion.

"At first it was for money. She was going to pay me five thousand. I couldn't go through with it. I was starting to like you. Joy, I'm sorry but you got to believe me."

Joy wanted to believe him but she knew that she could never trust him. The feeling of worthlessness consumed her. She knew nothing would ever be different for her. She would never have the feeling of complete happiness.

Daron was still driving. Neither one of them had any idea where they were.

Without further thought, Joy grabbed the wheel, causing him to lose control and run smack dead into a Dunkin Donut's. The last thing] Joy saw was a blinding light as she felt glass tear into her face, neck and arms. There was an intense shooting pain through her body then she felt nothing as darkness engulfed her.

Two and a half years passed since that night and Joy thought about it everyday. She had no choice and it served as a huge reminder. Daron walked away with no injuries. Joy was paralyzed from the waist down and had to serve a life sentence for causing the accident that killed a father of three children. The car not only hit the side of the building but a man standing in front of it.

"Williams, you have a visit."

Surprised, Joy rolled herself towards the visiting room. No one ever came to visit her. She didn't even have anyone listed, so she knew that it was probably a mistake. She would get down there and they would tell her to go back.

When she rolled through the door she thought she was hallucinating. On the other side of the glass stood Kevin, holding a little girl's hand. She was a spit image of herself and Joy knew right away that the girl was her daughter. Kevin had a long scar from the top of his head all the way down under his chin.

Joy was speechless. She couldn't stop staring as the correctional officer moved the chair closer.

"Kevin? I thought you were dead," she cried. She looked from him to the little girl and back at him.

"Almost. I was shot twice in the head. I was in a coma for six months. When I came out of it, I had to learn how to do everything again."

"Oh my God. Was that you who kept calling me?"

"That was me," he wiped the tears running down his face with the back of his hand.

"Is this...?" Joy stopped; she realized that she didn't know her own daughter's name.

He nodded his head, 'Her name is Aminah."

"Aminah," Joy repeated, looking down at her daughter. The little girl hid behind Kevin, sneaking peeks at Joy, "How did you find her?"

"It was hard. When I got better. I tried to find you. I hired a private investigator. He couldn't locate you at first but did found out that you had a baby that you abandoned at the hospital. After hearing that, I hired a lawyer to get custody of Aminah. I had to take a DNA test and once it showed that I was her father, custody was awarded to me."

Joy was stunned.

"When the PI told me that he found you and where you were, I debated for months whether I should come up here. I almost didn't come but I wanted you to see what you will miss out on. You see this beautiful child you threw away?" Anger creped into his voice.

"But Kevin I thought you were dead," Joy screamed in anguish.

"You can continue to think that because from this day forward, you will never see or speak to me or her again." Kevin got up, picked up their daughter and walked out the room.

Joy watched them leave and the thought hit her that the real reason for her unhappiness was her selfishness.

CHAPTER 27

(Alternate Ending)

An intense feeling of regret overcame Joy. She couldn't believe what she walked away from. She should have loved her child enough, not abandoned her. Joy never wanted to be like her mother but realized that she was just like her.

The longer she sat, the more the pain pierced her heart began to overwhelm her. What would her daughter think? Would she feel the same as Joy felt for her mother?

After Joy woke up in the hospital and found out she was going to jail and would never walk again. She thought jail was the lowest moment in her life but this was far worst. Joy chalked up her situation as being karma from all the bad things she'd done. She didn't feel like she wanted to die. Seeing Kevin with their daughter was too much for her to deal with. It was like she was being smacked in the face with all the regrets and disappointments that happened throughout her life.

When she closed her eyes, the moment Kevin and Aminah walked in the visiting room replayed through her head, she couldn't help herself. She felt the pain grow inside.

Joy knew she couldn't face her time after seeing what she could have had on the outside. So many ideas ran through her mind. She thought to escape but forgot her current crippled condition.

Hours passed and she still couldn't come up with anything that would help her. That night she couldn't sleep. She sat in the dark and thought about her little girl. She imagined that she was there with her. That she was in her life from the beginning. Joy realized that she had to change and she could make that happen.

The next morning, after breakfast, she used the phone to call her father's lawyer, Mr. Greco. She knew that he would sympathize because of how she lost her mother and father and her being paralyzed.

She told him about the accident that landed her in wheel chair and in jail. She explained how a man was killed when hit by the car. Leaving out the part that she was responsible for all of it, she made herself come off as a victim. He was silent. Joy wasn't sure he even listened but she continued.

"When I found out I would never walk again I didn't try to fight the charges against me. I wasn't driving the car," she pleaded.

"Wow. I don't know what to say," he said when Joy was done.

"Do you think you can help me get out of here?"

"I have to call around and get someone on your case. I'm only an estate lawyer. It may take a while but I'll get back to you."

Joy hung up the phone feeling a more hope than before the meeting. She wanted to change and become a better person, but she had to commit this one last act of her former self to get out of jail.

A few weeks passed and Joy had not heard anything from Mr. Greco. Then one day she was called down for a visit with her lawyer. She was surprised to see Mr. Greco sitting at the table along with a light skinned black woman. She was thin, pretty and she sat straight up in the chair. She looked very uncomfortable like she didn't want to be there.

She pushed her glasses closer to her face and spoke first. "Hi Joy. My name is Karen Brister. I'll be your lawyer through your appeal. Do you have any questions so far?"

She waited for Joy response; Joy shook her head no.

She continued, "I need to know everything that happened the night of the accident."

Joy looked at Mr. Greco. He slouched in his chair silent. He nodded at Joy to begin talking.

"Well, I don't remember much of what happened."

"It's okay. Just try to tell me what you do remember."

"I went with Wayne to his house. We had dinner and then we both became sleepy. I remember we went into his room and before I knew it, I was asleep."

"At what point did you leave the residence?"

"I woke up first and went into the living room. I looked through the DVD's for something to watch. I came across some homemade videos. I looked through them and noticed they all had the names of different women written on them." Joy paused and lowered her head. They both were looking at her with extreme intensity. Joy had to take a minute because she had to be believable. When she lifted her head, she had tears in her eyes.

"Take your time Joy." Mr. Greco said.

"I found one with my name on it. So I put it in. I watched as he laid me down in the bed. I was passed out. He raped me," she said, breaking down.

Mr. Greco came over to Joy and rubbed her back. "Joy then what happened?" he asked, his voice just above a whisper.

"I took the tape and woke him up. I demanded he take me home. I didn't tell him I knew about the tape until we were in the car. That's when he flipped out and crashed the car. He blamed everything on me. I plead not guilty but I barely paid attention to what was going on. I gave up."

"Joy do you still have the disk? Ms. Brister asked.

"It should be with my clothes and the other stuff I brought in here with me."

"First I want to do some more research into what happened in the case, then I see where to go from there. I'm going to see if I can locate the disk. When I know something I'll get back to you within the next couple days," she gathered her stuff and walked out the room.

Mr. Greco patted Joy's shoulder, giving her a feeling of hope before following Ms. Brister out the door.

Two months passed by. Ms. Brister kept contact with Joy letting her know the what she was doing and the progress she'd made; which wasn't much. Joy was beginning to get discourage. She decided to give up, and go with plan B.

She waited for lights out. She took out the razor she kept for protection. The plan was to slit her wrist; giving her enough time for her to bleed out before anyone can come and find her. By morning, she still hadn't find the courage to slit her wrist.

Another plan formed in her head as she watched the guards walk the block. She was focused on one in particular. CO. Pierce. He was short and stocky. He was light skinned, with a baldhead. He had beady eyes and a wide face that made him resemble a snake.

Joy decided to skip breakfast and stay on the block to talk to the CO. When she seen him walk back by her, she called out to him.

"Is there a problem Williams?"

"No. I was wondering if you could do something for me."

"It depends on what I get in return," he said, a goofy smile on his face.

"I need some sleeping pills. What will that cost me?"

"It'll cost you some head."

"That's it?"

"Yeah, but I want to watch you swallow my nut."

Joy was disgusted by the thought but she agreed.

"Put in a request to go to the hospital tomorrow. I will be the one to take you. We can do everything then," he said and disappeared.

Joy spent the rest of the morning in deep thought. Late in the afternoon, she got called down to meet with her lawyer. Her heart pounded harder and harder in her chest as she made her way down there.

When she saw Ms. Brister sitting at the table alone. Joy couldn't read her expression and thought it was bad news because Mr. Greco wasn't with her. Ms. Brister told her that she would receive a new trial and be released to a half way house.

Tears of joy ran down her face. She learned that she would leave tomorrow morning. She didn't know how she was going to make in the real world again, especially in a wheel chair.

CHAPTER 28

The van picked her up outside the jail and dropped her at the halfway house. It wasn't as bad as Joy thought it would be. The lady that ran the house was nice, she explained the rules. It was easy for Joy to get around and she had a room on the first floor, the bathroom down the hall. Joy could do everything herself. She could lift into bed or into her chair. There was a shower chair for her to shower. She felt better knowing she still could do things for herself. Joy was one of many in a wheelchair that lived at the house, a ramp built off the side of the porch.

For the first couple of days, Joy got used to living on the outside. When she figured how to get around on the bus, she went out. Curfew was at 7pm. Joy got up early the next morning. The bus picked her up down the block and she was off.

The bus took little time to drop her at the destination. Everything was still the same, but Joy hadn't thought through a plan, she couldn't get up the stairs in her wheelchair. She didn't see Kevin in the shop.

She climbed out her chair onto the first step. She pulled herself up the stairs until she was at the top. Her arms were tired and she could barely lift them to knock on the door. After giving herself some time to rest, she knocked.

A tall white man answered the door. "Yes how can I help you?" he asked, looking down at Joy with a look of confusion. He looked down at the wheelchair at the bottom of the stairs, "Are you okay? Do you need help?"

"No. Someone I used to know lived here. I thought he still lived here."

"I started renting the store and apartment. Nobody lived here for a while before I moved in." He continued to stare at Joy.

"Do you need help getting back down?"

"No. I'm sorry to bother you. I can get back down." Tears streamed down her face. She wasn't sure she could make it back down; she'd never done it before.

"You sure?"

"Yes." Joy said, in a low whisper.

The man stood there a few seconds longer before he went back inside. Grabbing the rail, Joy pulled her body to the edge and dropped down to the next step. She continued until she was four-steps from the top. As she dropped down to the next step, her hand slipped and she slid down the steps. She grabbed the rail but fell forward and tumbled down the remaining stairs.

She could do nothing but lay there. The man that answered the door came running down the steps with a phone to his ear. She watched as he felt for her pulse but she didn't feel his touch; her entire body was numb. He shouted something at her but she couldn't hear. Soon after, an ambulance came and took her to the hospital.

The doctors and nurses worked fast as soon as they surrounded her. Finally, the doctor gave her something for pain and knocked her out. When she awoke, the nurse who was changed her IV exited the room and returned with the doctor.

"Hi Ms. Williams. It's nice to see you're with us. I'm Dr. Robertson. Your surgery was successful. We removed a piece of bone from your lower back. It was pressed against some nerves in your back, causing your inability to walk. At the time it was seen as detrimental to remove it because of the risk it posed to causing further damage. It seems to have broken off and away without causing any additional damage."

"So, can I might walk?" Joy interrupted.

"Well, only time will tell. We still have to wait for the swelling to go down and for your staples to be removed. Let me take a look." he said, removing the blanket away from her legs.

"Can you move your toes?"

Joy looked down at her toes. She concentrated on moving them but nothing happened.

"Shit," Joy screamed, mad for getting her hopes up to began with.

"Don't get discouraged. It's going to take some time. Once you heal, you'll start physical therapy. For now, try not to worry and get better."

The doctor continued to examine Joy's legs and feet. He took a look at her staples and had the nurse change her bandages, then left.

Joy called her lawyer and let her know what happened. Ms. Brister told her she would handle everything at the halfway house.

EPILOGUE

Recovery took eight months of pain and hard work but Joy was able to walk again. She had a slight limp and needed to use a cane. Her new trial went smoothly. Joy was found not guilty on all counts. The prosecutor was upset but there was talk of going after Wayne for the charges and the added rape in the first degree. The DVD helped Joy look like more of a victim.

Joy got her GED and obtained a bachelor's degree in Behavior Health. Using the money she had left, Joy started a center for single parent families. The center hosted an after school program, parenting classes for teen parents and cooking classes. Counselors helped people addicted to alcohol, drugs and sex to overcome abusive relationships. Joy wanted to do everything in her power to help those with mental illnesses.

The center was successful in the community that Joy received thousands an additional $100,000 in funding to keep it running. Joy received media attention from the local news stations.

Joy sat at her desk looking over her notes about the homeless shelter when she heard a familiar voice.

"I didn't believe it when I saw you on television. Did you really do all this?"

"Yes," Joy managed to get out before her face flooded with tears. She looked at Kevin standing in the door way and thought she was dreaming. Since the day she last saw him and their daughter, not a day went by she didn't think of them.

"And you can walk?"

"Yeah."

"That's all you have to say?"

Joy wiped her tears and her face became wet again. She looked into Kevin's face and he smiled. He stepped forward and for the first time Joy noticed Aminah was hiding behind him.

"I have someone who wants to meet her mother," he said, moving over so Joy could see Aminah. She looked at Joy with a shy smile and waved.

Art Official Media Order Form
www.ArtOfficialMedia.com

Inmates ONLY get novels for $10.00 per book!

Titles	Prices
Blackface	$14.95
Blackface (CD Soundtrack)	$9.99
One Hundred Miles and Running (Blackface 2)	$14.95
Doughboy	$14.95
Lonely Hearts	$14.95
Nookie	$14.95
Nookie's Secret	$14.95
Tre Pound	$14.95
Tre Pound 2	$14.95
Blacktop Hustlaz	$14.95

Add $2.00 per book for shipping and handling.

Art Official Media LLC – PO Box 39323 – Baltimore MD 21212

Name ______________________________
Address ______________________________
City/State ______________________________
Contact # or email ____________________

Allow 3-5 business days for delivery. Art Official Media LLC is not responsible for prison orders rejected

Visit website http://www.ArtOfficialMedia.com for digital editions or download on Kindle, Nook or IPad.

CPSIA information can be obtained at www.ICGtesting.com
Printed in the USA
BVOW071840160212

283078BV00001B/4/P